K1602

O.P.

$6\frac{50}{AH}$

SCENES OF CHILDHOOD

SCENES OF CHILDHOOD

SYLVIA

TOWNSEND WARNER

THE VIKING PRESS · NEW YORK

First published in 1982 by The Viking Press
625 Madison Avenue, New York, N.Y. 10022

Library of Congress Catalog Card Number: 81–51529
ISBN: 0–670–62043–2

Printed in Great Britain

Set in 'Compugraphic' Baskerville

ACKNOWLEDGMENTS

With the exception of 'Siegfried on the Rhine' and 'In Pimlico', published here for the first time, all these stories appeared originally in *The New Yorker* between 1936 and 1973.

CONTENTS

Wild Wales

AFTER the eruption of Mont Pelée, the volcanic dust made its way even into our English skies, and imparted such extraordinary brilliancy to the sunsets that my mother found her paintbox quite inadequate until she thought of sending to Winsor & Newton for a supply of a paint called *rose dorée*. *Rose dorée* did the trick. It was unlike her to be caught thus unprovided. Before our summer holiday in Wales, with mountains and hydrangeas in mind, she laid in so many tubes of cobalt, ultramarine, and cerulean that I, too young to have any geographical notions as to where we were going, knew for a certainty that Wales would be blue.

The other thing I knew beforehand was that Nannie Blount would be there — a Brown Tree in the azure scene. By no exercise of faith or fancy could Nannie Blount be assorted to any shade of blue. Even indigo was too aerial for her.

Yet if it had not been for Nannie Blount, I daresay we should not have been going to Wales. When Johnnie Blount and I were still in our perambulators (Blount was, in fact, the name of Nannie's employers, and for all I know her real surname was Bones or Gridiron), she cast a bleak eye of approval on my nannie, who was a mere Florence. As they remained friends, Johnnie and I saw a great deal of each other. This entailed friendly relations between our mothers, and eventually between our fathers, so that by the time Johnnie and I were rising seven, it was natural and convenient — Nannie Blount having no objection — that the Blounts, who had rented a holiday house in Wales, should

1

ask us to stay with them. Mrs. Blount and my mother would do some sketching; Mr. Blount and my father would go fishing; jointly, all four would climb Cader Idris and go for bicycling excursions; and Johnnie and his little sister Amabel and his cousin Hugh, whose parents were in India, and I would play together while Nannie Blount and Florence, God willing, continued to enjoy each other's society.

Obviously, it cannot have rained every day of that visit, for days stand out in my memory — like the day we buried Amabel, like the day the cow chased the donkey — when the mountains behind us were without illusion, and the turf was crisp and dry under our bare feet, and our parents came bicycling home in the twilight with the skin peeling off their noses. But my general recollection is of a dramatic wateriness. There was a waterfall in the grounds of the house, which dashed all one's waking hours with a sense of wetness and vehemence. There were steaming morning mists, when the garden was full of rainbows, and the wasps in the fuchsia hedge were too languid to do anything but lie in wait to be injured and to repay. And there were the thunderstorms, which by some compact between the heavens and the mountains always broke over us when the wagonette had decanted us at some ideal site for painting and picnicking. (Unless, perhaps, there was some wild Welsh sorcery about the wagonette itself, which was kept in a shed behind the post office, embowered in ramparts of hydrangeas, whence it would emerge, dragged complaining from its repose, like some black Methodist Merlin.)

A wagonette, I had better explain, is a sort of genteel tumbril, massive, and vertiginously high. The occupants climb into it from the back, and sit on either side, exposed to the elements and staring into each other's doomed faces, while the driver, whose seat is even higher, turns an impersonal back on them and gives his mind to the horses. His legs are protected by a tarpaulin rug with metal-bound eyelets at each corner, through which it is hooked on to the vehicle, and a similar tarpaulin rug is laid over the laps of the passengers. This, if it rains, collects the rain in a puddle, and sometimes, by exquisite management, the puddle can be shot out over the back; otherwise, it accumulates until by some undisciplined movement it pours into somebody's lap.

But it was never raining when we set out. Sun flashed from the various metal fixings, flies hovered round our heads, cracks in the leather seats ossified, as we moved with the smell of hot horses through the smell of hot bracken, slowly, ponderously, and uphill, seeing, over stone walls laced with brambles and tufted with ferns, small fields full of ragwort, outcrops of stone, pigs feeding and sheep reposing, solitary whitewashed farms with more hydrangeas and rich-stinking middens, berried mountain ashes, hurrying brooks, and sudden disclosures of the sea, always so much farther up the sky than one expected. The wagonette creaked, the picnic basket rattled, the distant views grew ever bluer and more spectacular, horseflies joined the other flies, and it all took a very long time. Finally, we would reach the appointed place of sacrifice. The picnic basket and the lesser Isaacs would be lifted out, and there before us, basking in sunshine, would be the ideal site for painting and picnicking, usually with a waterfall but sometimes with a lake and invariably with crags. And then the coachman would unharness the two horses and go away with them to some farm, where he would find refreshment for man and beast. The tarpaulin rugs would be spread out for the children to sit on, and white enamel mugs and plates would be unpacked from the basket, with sandwich boxes and cake tins and bottles of milk and the large white enamel teapot and the spirit lamp. For after driving for so long in such heat and through such clouds of dust, everybody would be dying of thirst. When this had been done, and the matches mislaid and found again once or twice, the spirit lamp would burn with a blue flame, and the kettle, filled from the waterfall or the lake, would be beginning to boil. But faster than kettle could boil, anvil-shaped clouds would rise behind the crags, and a low rumble would be heard, and Mrs. Blount, in the apologetic tones of the hostess, would say, 'I hope that isn't a thunderstorm,' and my mother, in the cheerful tones of the guest, would reply, 'I expect it will pass over.' And a crash of thunder would smite the lie from her lips, and the first heavy drops of rain would fall, spotting the sandwiches, and a minute later everything would be wincing under flashes of lightning and then obliterated in a grey fury of rain, and Johnnie and Amabel and Hugh and I would be huddled away under the tarpaulin rug, with Nannie Blount telling Johnnie that if he as much as peeped out, the lightning would strike him. I often peeped out, hoping to see the lightning strike Nannie Blount. By then, everyone else was huddled under the wagonette, but Nannie was always beside us, a cloaked grey unblasted monolith, devoted to duty and waiting to catch poor Johnnie.

Mountain storms are quickly over. Long before the coachman came back with the horses, we were on top of the rug again, eating moist pink jam sandwiches, while my mother, dauntless creature, might be snatching a quick impression of retreating clouds. I don't pretend that these picnics were not enjoyable, but there was a certain monotony about them, and though the storms were so quickly over, we knew that we had not heard the last of them; they would reappear that evening, when Nannie Blount would draw our attention to how narrowly we had been spared before she led us in thanksgiving for having got through another day—even if only in order to set out into the perils of darkness, during which Satan would undoubtedly prowl, and the Almighty, as like as not, come as a thief in the night.

I can't believe that those amiable Blounts had any idea of the religious blackmail that went on in their nursery. They rejoiced in having such a faithful, trustworthy, old-fashioned, Bible-Christian servant, and never suspected the old-fashioned fire and brimstone she was charged with. By blackmail I don't mean merely those poor starving children

4

who would be thankful to eat our steamed blackberry pudding whenever we boggled at finishing a plateful of warm magenta crusts strewn with purple dregs, or the assurances, if we had a giggling fit, that we should soon laugh on the other side of our faces. These were moral assertions, which children, being born humanists, check by observation of the grown-up world and take with a pinch of salt. There are no such defences against the supernatural, and it was the supernatural we were exposed to. In the morning, we had Morning Worship, to crush our spirits for the day. In the evening, we had Evening Worship, to rape our consciences before going to bed. The blinds were half drawn, the nursery cat was shut out, a cloth was hung over the canary cage. Everything possible was done to increase our sense of being meritless and unprotected. And when we were conveniently at her mercy, and Florence and the nurserymaid (there was, of course, a nurserymaid, for Nannie Blount was far too invaluable to do anything like real work) in attendance, Nannie would say, 'Let us gather at the footstool,' whistle up her Maker with a 'Suffer the little ones to come unto Thee,' and fall to work. First came readings out of various little goody books — gruesome themes wrapped in twaddling language — or anecdotes of good children who walked twenty miles to buy a Bible, developed spinal complaints, repeated hymns to drunkards, and died young, or of naughty children who climbed a tree to get an apple, told a lie, were eaten by wolves, and died young. After this we repeated a hymn ourselves, while Nannie sat licking her lips before her *aria di bravura*. This was a cross between a sermon and a scolding. In the morning, it dwelt on our fallen natures and went into the backslidings that might be expected of us during the day. In the evening, these backslidings were brought home to us and reviewed in the light of the Four Last Things — death, judgment, hell, and heaven — and a three-to-one odds against us. Then, when she judged we had been sufficiently thumped, she creaked down on her knees and laid it all before the Lord in a bloodcurdling tête-à-tête. Hugh

5

averred that he rather liked these ceremonies. He was born in India; no doubt he had Kali and Juggernaut in his blood. Amabel was too young to express an opinion. I, when I had got over their total novelty, groaned under them, and languished for the moment when Nannie would begin to pray, for during the tête-à-tête she knelt with her back to us, and I could count her hairpins. But what Hugh or I thought of them meant nothing to her. It was on Johnnie, a delicate sickly child and the apple of her eye, that she focused these burning-glass attentions.

Johnnie was fatally good, brave, honourable, guileless, and accident-prone. The dexterity he lavished on his accidents would have fitted out a circus. In one of our walks, I remember, we came to a place where a stream was channelled between two rims of masonry, less than a foot apart. Johnnie, with a mere pirouette, immersed himself at full length in that channel. If he went near a gooseberry bush, he disturbed a wasp nest. If he tripped, he fell headlong, and face downwards, and his nose bled. When his nose bled, it was always on a clean suit—the poor child was never out of clean suits. If he spoke with his mouth full, he choked. If he ran his finger over a propped-up bicycle, it fell on him. If he caressed a cat, it kittened. And for all these things his soul was required of him by Nannie Blount, who sent him to bed, stood him in the corner, set him down to do another six rows of penitential cross-stitch, browbeat him with God, and told him he had grieved Jesus.

Yet on the day when we buried Amabel, Johnnie was the cool conscienceless villain of the piece. We were on the beach, it was blazingly hot, and after telling us all the things we mustn't do Nannie told us to play nicely with Amabel while she had a little rest. After a while, Johnnie said, 'I think we'll bury Amabel now.' Infant burials were not unfamiliar to us; there were dozens of them in the goody books. So under Johnnie's direction we dug a deep grave, and made a little pillow at one end of it for Amabel's head; and since we couldn't line the grave with moss, we threw in some pretty bits of seaweed. Then Amabel was helped into

6

the grave and encouraged to lie still in it, and the sand we had dug out we shovelled in on top of her. The unskilled labour of burying Amabel's leg end was allotted to Hugh and me, while Johnnie spread out her curls on the pillow and patted sand over them. Thus weighted down at either end, Amabel became increasingly easy to bury, and though for some queer reason we all avoided burying her face, the rest of her was soon immobilized and her yells were so enfeebled that they would not have alerted a gazelle, much less Nannie Blount and Florence, who were sitting in the shade of a dune, telling horror stories, most likely—for besides the horror stories she dispensed for the nursery, Nannie Blount had a fine repertory of horrors for adult use, all of which had happened in her own experience, and these, of course, we constantly overheard. (Some I afterwards identified in the Newgate Calendar, others in the works of Mrs. Henry Wood, but others again, such as the story of the fire that broke out in the lunatic asylum, had every mark of being her own.) We went on heaping sand over Amabel, and Nannie Blount might soon have had another horror story to call her own if we had not heard a whistle, looked round, and seen a man and a dog coming along the beach. The man was not a Black Man, the dog did not have blue fire coming out of its mouth, there was no sign that they had been sent to carry us away. But the sight of them suddenly smote us into common sense, and we promptly unburied Amabel, and hauled her from the grave, and shook the sand out of her clothes, and did what we could to restore her curls. She was very hot to the touch, and at first rather dazed, and then rather peevish. But she was none the worse for it. Neither, for that matter, were we. Our consciences as the noonday clear, since the man and the dog had gone past us without comment, we resumed our nice play. And though the day ended with the usual analysis of what we had done wrong in it, and the usual saddening reflections on what we might expect if we died in our sleep, I don't think any of us felt any special conviction of sin, and if we did, we certainly didn't mention it.

Many years afterwards, I met a middle-aged Amabel, peaceful, wise, and great, like Swift's Dorothea, and was so shocked to think that we had nearly murdered her that I apologized for my share in the business. She did not remember it, though she dimly remembered the thunderstorms and the wasps in the fuchsia hedge. Then we talked about Johnnie, who was killed in 1917. Children driven good are apt to be driven mad. It was that approach to mass madness which still makes me feel slightly sick when I remember the day we buried Amabel. But the day when the cow chased the donkey is a memory of unspotted bliss.

A belt of salt meadow lay between us and the seashore. It extended so far on either hand, with here and there a tumbled stone wall, and the wandering idle course of the little river that ran so vehemently through our garden, and herds of small black cattle feeding, that even to traverse it seemed a long adventure. Hugh, our elder, could walk the distance easily enough, Amabel was jolted across it in a gocart, but Johnnie and I were inclined to lag behind and be a nuisance, and, our nurses complaining of this, someone had the ideal of hiring a donkey in the village that was accustomed to be harnessed with panniers and used for bringing up loads of seaweed. It knew the way to the beach as if it had been born there, the owner said, and was so good-hearted that you could guide it with a rush. All this, oddly enough, proved true. Johnnie and I, strapped into our panniers, bobbed along, conversing across the donkey's steep back, and the donkey's good-heartedness was such that even though Nannie Blount persisted in walking beside it, goading it with her white cotton umbrella, it showed no resentment and paid no attention.

Why, on that particular day, that particular black cow should have felt that particular animus is not the sort of thing one can explain — though when my mother heard about it afterwards (for on that particular day our parents were away bicycling, or climbing Cader Idris, perhaps, for they did eventually climb it), she assured me that the poor cow had lost its calf and was therefore not responsible

8

for its actions. Anyhow, the cow suddenly detached itself from its friends, burst into our little cavalcade, and began to chafe its horns against my pannier. The donkey very sensibly broke into a trot, the cow uttered some morose lows, and there the matter would probably have ended if Nannie Blount had not felt she must dominate the brute creation and so aimed a whack at the cow. The cow made a sally at her, changed its mind, and ran after the donkey. The donkey continued to trot, the cow lumbered beside it, and Nannie followed in pursuit, grim as Nemesis, and whacking everything within range, as I have observed implacable Nemesis often does herself. At last, smiting with all her force, she broke the white cotton umbrella across the donkey's rump. Good-hearted, mild, and court-eous as that donkey may have been, it was a Welsh donkey; it could not stomach injustice. It put back its ears and started to gallop. The cow, too, however weighed on by maternal grief, was a Welsh cow, neither to be bested by a donkey nor deterred by a broken umbrella, and the cow's friends, Welsh to a cow, were not going to stand ingloriously by. They joined in the pursuit. Then the first cow — by now, so to speak, our own cow — turned back and by a dextrous cutting-out movement isolated Nannie, and deflected her course. She ran, but she did not run alone. Leaning out of our panniers, we saw with amazement, with stupor, with inexpressible rapture and delight, Nannie in full flight, and all the cows chasing after her. We had never imagined that the righteous judge, the harbinger of the last and dreadful day, the searcher into all hearts, and the vicaress of God could run so fast.

Meanwhile the donkey galloped on seawards, and I could not but remember an anecdote (against wilfulness) in one of the goody books, about a lady in a donkey chaise whose donkey would not draw her over the sands because it was alarmed by the sight of the waves, whereon the lady got out, tied her shawl over its head, got into the chaise again, and whipped up the donkey, who incontinently rushed into the sea, where they both drowned. A like fate seemed imminent

9

for us; but if in our last moments we could still watch the spectacle of the cows chasing Nannie, and Florence and the nurserymaid chasing the cows, as they were now doing, it would be worth it. And as I have never seen the windy plains of Troy, I see them in my mind's eye looking exactly like that expanse of green salt meadows, so flat and timeless and self-sufficient, over which scurried those distant figures, and whence the offshore breeze carried to us the sound of thundering hoofs and the wailing cries of women. However, when our donkey got among the sand hills, it stopped. By that time, all was over, for we had seen Nannie, apparently hoisted on horns, scrambling over a stone wall, and the cows, whose joy was in the chase, quietly dispersing, and Florence and the nurserymaid climbing the wall unassisted, and Hugh, wheeling Amabel in the gocart, coming to join us and whistling as he came.

This, I am glad to say, was not all. For it turned out that we were not the only persons to see Nannie in flight. She had been watched from the village, too. Civil inquiries, expressions of sympathy, congratulations on her speed, and even on her legs, greeted her return; but the general sense was pretty plain, and found expression in 'Run away from the cows? Dear, dear! Ra-ther sil-ly.'

When our visit ended, Florence went off for her fortnight's holiday, and the wagonette — but this time without a thunderstorm, since no picnic was involved — took us to a farm farther along the coast, where a Mrs. Jones let lodgings. My parents had found it for themselves, while exploring on their bicycles, and had been much taken with it, and even more taken with Mrs. Jones — rightly, for she was a dear old woman, hale and light-footed, the soul of kindness, and the body of kindness, too. Musing on the discrepancy between Mrs. Jones and Nannie Blount, and on what could be accountable for it, I said to my mother, 'Are all Christians cross?' My mother, who thought that small children should be given honest answers, replied, 'No. Not all of them.' I took her word for it, and dived back into my native paradise of being a solitary and unprayed-over child.

10

My days began with picking mushrooms for breakfast, mushrooms so newly out of the turf that shreds of dry moss and dewy blades of grass still adhered to them. I watched the cows milked and the pigs fed. I wound rushes into bracelets and plaited them into hatbands, and tried — and sometimes succeeded for as much as a couple of inches — to peel the green hide off the white pith, having learned about rushlights from Mrs. Jones, who still used them. I followed dragonflies along the ditches, and hunted for four-leaf clovers, and laid out gardens of pebbles and flower heads, and combed a deserted rubbish heap for bits of broken pottery and coloured glass, and horseshoes, and old medicine bottles Veniced by age and weather, and inestimable kettles and frying pans with only quite small holes in them. When I was tired of playing out-of-doors I went to visit Mrs. Jones in her kitchen, where there was always something interesting going on — damsons being made into jam, bullace cheeses being put away on the top shelf of the pantry, mushrooms being pickled, knives sharpened, butter churned, beans sliced, raisins stoned, the clock being wound or the dresser beeswaxed. The oak dresser was black with age and took up the whole of one wall, and the ceiling was oak-panelled, too, but the room seemed rich, rather than dark, for it was full of things that were bright in themselves, like the lustre jugs and the japanned trays, or that were polished to brightness. Photographs of Mrs. Jones' relations and of school treats and choir outings, all with cheerful stories attached, hung in patterns on the walls; there were two tabby cats and a collie and a harmonium and patchwork cushions and jelly moulds and ornamental canisters; and an iron chain with a hook hung down the chimney. And with all this richness and variety went the richness and variety of the smells: the smell of beeswax, of new bread, of smoked bacon, of apples, and cloves, and vinegar, and the geraniums in the window and the water peppermint that kept flies away, and of Indian tea and blackberries — blackberries not miserably stewed but baked in the oven with all their dark velvety fragrance preserved to

11

them. Mrs. Jones was an oven cook, and part of the pleasure of her kitchen was the thought of all the different things cooking behind the massive black-leaded door with a rose embossed on it, and the delicious anticipation of when she would open that door to take something out and put something else in.

It was disconcerting when, in the midst of all my bliss and freedom and security, and with so much still to enjoy — for we had only been there a little over a week — I found I could not enjoy anything because my legs felt so unreal and my head so heavy and my throat so sore. I was put to bed, and almost at once the bed began to change its dimensions and to wander about the room, while its brass knobs grew larger and larger, and then grew small again, and far away. In the morning, I was told that my father had gone to fetch a doctor and a pineapple. As I understood it, there was going to be a dinner party; not till Mrs. Jones prescribed it had my parents known the efficacy of pineapple for an inflamed throat.

My poor father bicycled for twelve miles to the nearest doctor, a bottle-nosed veteran with a stately port. When he heard where we were staying, he said 'H'mph!' When he heard my symptoms, he said 'Ha!' Growling to himself, he disappeared into a filthy cupboard, where he could be heard taking down bottles and shaking up medicines. Reappearing, he said, 'And what on earth possessed you to take a child to that pesthouse? It's notorious; everyone knows about it.'

'Nobody told us.'

'I should hope not. Do you expect decent people to take the bread out of a widow's mouth? You should have asked me!' he exclaimed.

Having thoroughly rolled on his Englishman, he said briskly that the dogcart would be ready in five minutes and that my father had better ride with him. He drove furiously, and enlivened the journey with stories of legendary local cesspits.

I remember nothing of that first visit, when he qualified

my sore throat by the eighteenth-century term of putrid, won my mother's heart by his good manners and then told her she must have that tooth out, and descended to sit in Mrs. Jones kitchen, where he smoked a cigar and drank several cups of tea. It was later that he won my heart, telling me that I gargled like a lion. He won my heart, and I have been given to understand that he saved my life, but all I can remember of him is that one remark and the cheerful tramp of his boots as he approached the house. The only distinct and unequivocal recollection I retain from that illness is of a sunset I saw from my window. There was a mackerel sky, with innumerable small clouds, close-packed as pebbles on a beach, and a flaming scarlet light gradually extended through them, till the whole western sky up to the zenith seemed to be on fire, interminably brightening and never consumed, while over this formal splendour the vapours left by an equinoctial storm hurried, cringing and distraught. If I had been more susceptible, if Nannie Blount had had her will of me, I should have watched this hell-fire sunset with different eyes. As it was, I saw it as being exactly like the pain in my throat.

The Poodle, the Supernatural,
Mr. Wilson, Mr. Tatos,
and My Mother

WHEN my parents took me to stay with Cousin
Ursula, I was not told that her house was
reputed to be one of the best-haunted houses
in Ireland. Cousin Ursula was my first cousin twice
removed—removed, that is, by two generations—and
as I was seven at the time, I daresay they thought I
was not ripe for ghosts. We spent three weeks at Castle
Pink; most of the time it rained, and this blurred my
impressions, for one wet day in a large country house in
which you are the only child is much like another. How the
gooseberries were arranged for dessert is perhaps what I
remember most clearly, and the butler's tense, pale face as
he set the edifice on the table. This needed concentration
and a steady hand, for they were arranged on a wide, long-
stemmed platter, first a pavement of red gooseberries, then
a pavement, one gooseberry less in diameter, of green
gooseberries, and so on in a diminishing striped red-and-
green cone till the summit was topped off with a single
gooseberry, red or green as came uppermost. Whether this
was a traditional Irish way of arranging gooseberries or
whether Cousin Ursula had ordained it because she liked
that kind of Italian architecture, I can't say; I have never
seen its like elsewhere, and I have never had enough large,
smooth, princely gooseberries to imitate it myself. I remember, too, with deep affection and intimacy, a sedan chair
that I spent a great deal of my time in. All children like
dens, most children like sumptuosity, and I lurked in the
sedan chair, delightfully conscious that the outside of my
den was gilded and painted, and that its inside was padded,

dusky, and smelled both mildewy and aromatic. The sedan chair stood in a hall as wide as a church nave, and one winter night (as I was told long after) rats moved it half across the floor, while other rats rang every bell in the house and trampled like the constabulary.

I have never sat in a sedan chair since. When we were on our way home and the boat began to move down the Liffey, my mother exclaimed, 'Never again, George! Never, never again!' For though she had been spared the Red Room, which was so notorious that only the toughest bachelors or chance members of the Royal Family were expected to sleep in it, and though the Blue Room had challenged her with nothing more positive than a noise like a horse, she said, sighing its heart out, invisible hands sporting with her hair-brushes, and half a dozen barefooted men wrestling in the adjacent dressing-room, she had been cowed by the general mood of acquiescent panic that prevailed through the house; by the fact that the housemaid bringing hot-water cans or what not to the bedroom was always two house-maids, clinging to each other; that guests came down to breakfast looking as though they had been dragged through hell backwards; that conversations were kept going not merely with the usual social obligation to keep up talk but desperately, as if a silence were an invocation to Pande-monium; that everyone went about glancing behind him, listening with one ear for something unspecified, showing strong reluctance to move about the house alone and abject panic at the prospect of going to bed—everyone, that is, except Cousin Ursula. She herself looked like a spectre, but the spectre of a camel, for she was extremely tall and thin and walked with a camel's swaying rawboned gait. Rats, according to her, accounted for half of it, and the other half was no more than one would expect in a country that had been mismanaged for centuries. For she was absorbed, as only an Englishwoman could be, in doing her duty to Ireland. She studied the Irish language, bought tweeds, and brooches of the targe-like proportions associated with what was then called the Celtic Twilight, encouraged creameries, combatted tuberculosis, and scoured the land on a bicycle, lecturing about open windows and Home Rule.

Though we evaded any more visits to her particularly inspissated twilight ('. . . and make it a good *long* stay, for if the crossing makes Sylvia sick, it would not be worth your while to come for a mere week'), we met whenever she came to London. She usually came over during an Abbey Theatre London Season, because it was restful to sit among an audience that felt no religious or patriotic call to riot in the pit, and she and my mother sometimes went out and hunted antiques together. It was a combination of antiques, finances, and rheumatism that finally persuaded her to spend a couple of years in Italy while Castle Pink was let to some profitable salmon fisher who might feel inclined to mend the roof. As such people always break everything they touch, the best of the furniture was to be distributed among museums and relations: would we mind housing a chair?

It was not, alas, the sedan chair—though by then I had outgrown the Den Age. It was a black oak armchair, of the type called Elizabethan, or, less specifically, massy, with an upright back and a great deal of carving—a stately object, and not altogether as uncomfortable as it looked. Though it was a great deal more stately than we were, and had a marked appearance of being itself well aware of this, and of stiffly moping over what a harsh fate had done to it, by the time my mother had revised her drawing-room, and led up to it with a Persian rug, and got rid of the old settee, and bought a more serious-minded wastepaper basket, it looked, we agreed, very creditable, and by no means as large as when first unpacked. Unfortunately, we had a poodle.

While the chair was still approaching us in its packing case, my mother had said, 'One thing is categorical. We cannot have the poodle sleeping in it. God knows how we shall discourage him, but discouraged he must be.' Our poodle combined a soft heart and an iron will, to a degree that only a hero of some popular Edwardian novel could have equalled, and it was plain from my mother's words that she was already laying some of the onus of discouragement on an all-powerful God, so that if the poodle slept in Cousin Ursula's chair, my mother would not be the only one to blame. No blame was incurred by either contracting party. When the armchair had been installed, and three or four cushions thrown into it to allay its aspect of sombre reluctance to settle down with us, the poodle was called in while my mother stood by in an easy, nonchalant attitude, looking categorical. The poodle caught sight of the chair, stopped dead, and shuddered to his foundations. Still shuddering, he cringed backwards to the farthest corner of the room. 'It must seem quite enormous to him,' said my mother. She spoke with her usual easy infallibility, but against the deepening background of the poodle's discouragement she sounded like a wren singing under a thundercloud. When the poodle abruptly hurled himself against the door, my father kindly let him out.

For some days, the poodle went on sitting just inside the door, even during teatime, but he gave up shuddering, and seemed resigned to snatching his piece of cake out of the air instead of getting it from my mother's hand. After a week or so, he even persuaded himself that there was no harm in coming as far as the hearthrug. It was from the hearthrug that he suddenly rose up one wet afternoon and advanced, walking slowly on stiff legs and growling under his breath, till he was almost within touching distance of the armchair. There he remained, his head stretched forward, his legs braced for attack, snuffing, and exhaling each snuff on a growl. I remarked to my mother that the chair seemed to be getting larger again. She replied briskly that it was a sad fate to have a daughter with adenoids. Hadn't I noticed that the chair, like everything else in that awful house, smelled of mildew? Naturally on a wet day like this the smell was stronger, so no wonder the poor dog objected to it. But whether she was defending the poodle or that handsome piece of furniture she was now embroidering a squab cushion for, I do not know. Neither of us felt inclined to interrupt the poodle. He was officially gentle as a lamb, but

17

he was larger than a lamb. When he had finished inhaling the smell of Castle Pink and saying what he thought of it, he came back to the hearthrug and lay down, looking as those do who have done their duty, however unavailingly— baffled, that is to say, and residually morose.

All this became quite a regular performance of his, and my mother took some pride in it. Like the chair itself, it was not the sort of thing you would find in every house. When people came to see us, they were told that it might happen while they were there, and if it did happen, if the night-blooming cereus opened its petals before their eyes, they were expected to enjoy it. It made no difference to the poodle, as my mother proudly insisted, whether or no the chair had someone sitting in it. He did not growl because he might presently bite, he hadn't a bellicose thought about him; he was more psychic than usual poodles, that was all. To show the truth of this, she would sit down on the lap of the ghost, or the mildew, or whatever it was that the poodle took exception to so interestingly, and, paying her no atten- tion whatsoever, he would keep up his hallucinated objur- gations. It was blood-curdling. It was, indeed, more blood- curdling, being less explicit, than my mother's accounts of staying at Castle Pink. But these also helped to entertain our duller visitors and to endear the chair. By the time she had finished embroidering its squab cushion, it was so deeply endeared that she had begun to think how empty her life and the poodle's would be when the time came for it to go back to Ireland. And what decided her to commission that flap-eared young Mr. Wilson to make one of his char- coal ghouls of her (Mr. Wilson was fresh from studying with Herkomer) was the realization that his strenuous technique would be perfect for the chair. So she would sit for her portrait in it, with the devoted poodle at her feet. Possibly the poodle's devotion would not stretch quite so far as this, but Mr. Wilson could easily make a separate study of him and put it in where it was wanted, like the Old Masters.

Having settled all this with the artist, she turned her energies to the next undertaking she had in mind, which

18

was orange gin. A dozen wide-mouthed, high-shouldered jars were bought, heaven knows how many oranges and how much rock candy, and two dozen bottles of gin — to be on the safe side — and carried up to what our house painter misguidedly referred to as Mrs. Warner's boudoir. (And when I think of the price of gin in those enskied days, I wonder how anyone of my generation can have the courage to write reminiscences.) I was breaking rock candy with a little mallet, my mother was humming 'Ouvre tes yeux bleus, ma mignonne' and packing her jars, the poodle was chewing the little tags of string the sugar had candied on, when a servant came in to say that Mr. Wilson was in the drawing-room.

'Drat the man! Of course he would be punctual,' said my mother. 'Sylvia, wash your hands and go down and entertain him while I just finish this jar and make myself presentable. Make some excuse or other. Wash them thoroughly!'

Mr. Wilson rose from the haunted chair as I entered. I begged him to be seated, and explained that my mother always lay down after lunch and was lying down now, but would come in a moment. How we got round from that to the Rokeby Venus, I do not recollect, but there was ample time to get there by any route, for a quarter of an hour had gone by before my mother came in, looking presentable, followed by the devoted poodle (who had also been made presentable, by the rapid running of a comb through his tufts), and moving in an aura of gin.

Again Mr. Wilson rose from the haunted chair; again he sank back into it. As he did so, the poodle rushed forward and clenched his teeth in what happened to be Mr. Wilson's trousers but might just as well have been Mr. Wilson's leg. Seizing him by his newly combed tufts, my mother and I dragged him away. My mother said it was unforgivable. Mr. Wilson said it was nothing, poor old boy, nothing. My mother reiterated that it was unforgivable, that she would have to speak to him severely, that her only consolation was that it would supply a job for dear Mrs. Hooper, who smocked and fine-darned though she was over eighty, and really Mr. Wilson should do a drawing of her — such wrinkles! Mr. Wilson said that he couldn't think of such a thing but that he really must meet Mrs. Hooper; Herkomer had taught him what one can find in wrinkles. He was about to sit down again when my mother tactfully diverted him towards the sofa, explaining that nothing was further from the poodle's natural disposition than to attack people; he was gentle as a lamb. It was the chair he attacked, for undoubtedly he saw some kind of ghost in it; the chair had come from a house in Ireland, etc. 'But sit anywhere else,' she concluded, 'and he won't harm a hair of your head.'

Mr. Wilson sat down on the sofa. The poodle rushed at him again, and bit him in the calf of the leg.

How Mr. Wilson got away in his trousers from my mother I really cannot say. But he did, and forgave us, and added her to his Ghouls' Gallery. She did not sit to him in the chair, however. Analysing the affair of Mr. Wilson's leg, she saw clearly what had gone wrong. Mr. Wilson should never have sat in it as if he had done it for weeks, as if it belonged to him. The poodle resented this as an impiety. You couldn't blame the poor animal for that; he was expressing his dumb version of a religious conviction, and was no worse than the Salvation Army or the Crusaders.

'Better than the Crusaders,' said my father. 'They slaughtered a whole zoo in Constantinople and ate most of it.'

'Did they really? The fiends! And then they go and lie on their backs in the Temple Church with their legs crossed, looking as smug as pork pies. Hypocrites!'

'Zealots, zealots,' said my father soothingly. 'Zealots are not always rational. What are you going to do about the chair — move it to the boxroom?'

'Move that splendid chair to the boxroom? And let loose all its ghosts or whatever they are to rage as they please in the attics? No, no! If there is a ghost in that chair, I'll keep it under my eye.'

'Very well, my dear. But people will sit in it.'

'No, they won't! I'll soon put a stop to anything of the

sort. Look—isn't it a lovely colour? I remembered in the night that I had it put away in a drawer.' My mother displayed several yards of heavy velvet ribbon, in her favourite shade of rose colour; and while we were still about to say that we didn't think the poodle would take to rose-coloured trappings, she looped it from one arm of the chair to the other and tied the ends in one of her inimitable bows.

'There! Just like the Victoria and Albert.'

Apparently the ribbon had some sort of exorcising effect for the poodle, for he paid no more attention to the chair, except when he rubbed his fleas against its carved legs. But other people coming into the room seemed taken aback. For a while, my mother remembered to explain; afterwards, they were left to think it out for themselves.

It was during one of her excursions to the Victoria and Albert Museum that my mother fell into conversation with a Mr. Tatos, who was admiring a mazer that she also admired. A man, and a connoisseur, he would have been whirled into subjection even if she had not known a mazer from a milk bowl; he asked her to go on with him to Christie's salesroom, and after that gave her tea at Barbellion's. Mr. Tatos's knowledge of antiques and works of art had awed and delighted my mother (she was, indeed, extremely humble and ready to learn whenever there was not a prior obligation to teach, direct, ordain, spring-clean, and generally keep us in order); she ordered *crème brulée* when he came to lunch. Mr. Tatos was a gliding, insubstantial man, dressed, with what my mother's French fashion paper called *une élégance discrète*, in a dark-brown suit and a mulberry-coloured tie. He had dark-rimmed eyes and a husky voice, and he looked at my mother as though he were an intensely musical cobra listening to the snake charmer's flute. As he entered the room, he caught sight of the chair (one could not avoid doing so), and he, too, appeared to shudder, though the shudder was suppressed. Then, much as the poodle had done, he went into a corner of the room, where he looked for some time at an oil painting.

21

'Mmm,' he said, a sad, soft, mewing sound. 'That's a very nice little Pater you've got there. I shouldn't think it's ever been taken out of that frame, either. Lovely, lovely!'

'It belonged to my grandfather,' she said. 'But I don't think he thought much of it.'

'Mmmmmm,' said Mr. Tatos, mewing even more wistfully. 'What a grandfather! Had a Pater in an original frame, thought nothing of it, never sent it to be skinned by a restorer, never had the frame brightened up with a lick of gold paint. What a grandfather! I never had grandfathers like that. That's a dear little bit of Capo di Monte. Very typical.'

'Is that Capo di Monte?'

After some valuable hints on Capo di Monte, Mr. Tatos paused before one of my mother's water colours, saying that it was a nice piece of colour, and that he could see she understood brown madder. He also had some flattering things to say about a cameo, about the fire irons, about a teapot that was certainly Lowestoft, about a bowl that as certainly wasn't, but was interesting, yes, very interesting. While my mother edged him up the room towards the chair, he, like the artist he was, reserved his moment of acclamation, delaying to say kind words about the meaner beauties of the drawing-room. Even when she had got him right up to the chair, he broke back for another study of the bowl that wasn't Lowestoft — Longton Hall, perhaps, mmm, and it looked to him as if it had once had a cover; had she noticed the little traces of wear on its rim? She'd see them very plainly if she'd use his magnifying glass. Did this come from the grandfather, too? Bought it at an old-clothes shop in Lichfield? Had she indeed? He must congratulate her. Three and sixpence? Gracious heavens!

'Take care of it,' he said beseechingly. 'I shouldn't keep those nutcrackers in it if I were you. Really I shouldn't.'

Brought face to face with the chair, he put his magnifying glass back in his pocket. He looked at it. It seemed to me that he was more attentive to the bow than to anything else. Be that as it may, he looked at the chair, and such was his control that the only sign of emotion that escaped him was a faint twiddling of his fingers.

'Did you buy this?' he asked, and his voice was sombre.

'No. It isn't even ours. We're just looking after it.'

'Thank God!' It was as if the cobra had come out of its trance and spoken like a human being. 'Thank God, I say! After that bowl you bought for three and sixpence, it would have broken my heart to think that anyone had sold you this mausoleum. Fifty years old at the most, and made in Belgium, at that.'

'I had doubts about it myself,' said my mother. He gave her another glance of devoted admiration, but this time it was plainly as from one cobra to another. Then we went in to lunch.

As soon as my mother could arrange for it (and she moved with speed when she wished to), the armchair, with all its supernatural associations but minus the rose-coloured velvet ribbon, went to a furniture repository. There was a little discussion between my father and my mother as to whether or not it should be insured, and if so, for how much. My father got his way; it was insured from Cousin Ursula's point of view, not Mr. Tatos's. This was fortunate, for within a month's time a fire broke out in the repository, and the chair was consumed. That is not quite the end of the story; many years later, Castle Pink, built of stone, un-inhabited, and standing in one of the wettest parts of Ireland, set itself on fire and was burned to the ground. No one will believe this, and no importance attaches to anyone's belief or disbelief. But it is true.

My Father, My Mother, the Butler, the Builder, the Poodle, and I

THOUGH I read startling pieces in newspapers about the impending Americanization of Britain, I remain seated: I have been through it once already. An early experience has shown me what course it will take. Glad surprise will be followed by some interesting turmoils, turmoils will bring on a state of apathy, and then it will all die down and sink mossily into the English landscape.

I was only ten years old when my father's schoolmastering career in an English public school brought him to the stage where he had to become a housemaster (this meant taking charge of an establishment that housed, fed, and loco-parentized about forty boys between the ages of fourteen and eighteen), but I shared in my parents' glad surprise at the amenities of our new residence. The previous house-master had, I think, visited the United States; at any rate he was conscious of them, for he had imported and installed a great deal of American equipment, which included twenty shower baths. At that date, the English bathed at full length; they warmed themselves before open fires; their staircases were wooden and inflammable; their passages were curly and draughty. But I need not expatiate. These conditions still persist, and bygonely-minded visitors even come to revel in them. Judge, then, how stimulating it was for the Warners to stray from radiator to radiator, to gaze down vistas of shower baths, to bask in warm corridors, and to keep off the besetting dread of fire, which haunts those who have to look after other people's children, by reposing on the thought of the wonderful American fire alarm that the gentleman before my father had recently had put in.

I cannot recall the name of this marvel, but I remember everything else about it. It ran like a vine through the house, with little contraptions in each room, and larger nodal contraptions at strategic points, and was based on the theory that metals expand when sufficiently heated. If fire broke out anywhere, there at its elbow was a little metal tongue, or lappet, or some such, that would expand, and this would send an electric impulse careering along the vine, or break a contact, or something. Anyhow, in the twinkling of an eye very loud gongs, integrated in the nodal contraptions, would begin to sound, and at the same moment a small flap — one of a dozen or so, each representing a region of the house — would fly open, displaying a baleful red eye on the façade of the nodal contraption, which was black and gold, about a foot and a half square, and guarded by a glass door. I hope I have made this clear.

One of these nodal contraptions was in the passage just outside my bedroom, and when we were newly in the house, I used, night after night, to get out of bed and stand watching it, praying in a blasphemous and unwomanly spirit that the gong might begin to sound and the little flap fly open. I had enjoyed this experience in blueprint already, for, naturally, my father had not been able to keep his hands off our marvel and had lit a match under one of the tongues, or lappets, experimentally. The result was wonderful, and I liked it very much, but it was not the real thing. The real thing could not properly take place unless I happened to be observing the nodal contraption when a real fire broke out.

A good deal of the house was old, full of woodwork, and perilous, so this made our fire alarm vitally gratifying, but there was also our American wing, built on by the previous gentleman in a modern and fire-resisting manner. Its stairs were stone, its floors were concrete, except for window frames and doors there was no woodwork about it. And no little coals could jump from the grate and set fire to a hearthrug, because there were no hearths, only radiators. A room that has no chimney, however, is not perfectly ventilated by a window alone. The architect of our American wing had supplied each room with a ventilator, a brick-sized cavity in the wall just above the door, closed on both sides by metal grids. Could providence go further?

Yet it was in this very American wing that the process of de-Americanization first showed itself as a possibility. In spite of the concrete floors and the faultless ventilation, our American wing began to harbour a smell. It was an odd kind of smell. Sometimes it was here, sometimes there; sometimes you could scarcely detect it, and at other times it was very strong indeed. It was my mother who ran it down. Thinking that a small boy in this wing was looking home-sick, she had gone to have a little loco-parentis chat with him, and while gazing around his room for something that might inspire her to further conversation (for he seemed constrained and tongue-tied), she happened to notice a moving obscurity in the ventilator. It was a rat, a pet rat. Its owner, finding that he could not always conveniently carry the rat about on his person, had picked loose the metal grid of his ventilator and made the rat a nice, safe cage, and this humane scheme had been adopted by other nature lovers in our American wing.

That happened in the summer term. Next term, when the winter was just getting into its stride, the boiler that fed the radiators developed a crack. That would have been nothing out of the common — boilers in schoolhouses are as fragile as butterflies — but this was a peculiar boiler, which had accompanied the radiators from the United States. Mr. Jessop, our builder, plumber, and decorator, reported that its pipes and appurtenances were so germane to it that no mere British boiler could take its place; there was nothing for it but to get a boiler from America. In those days, boilers were not sent about by air. During November and December, the radiators were out of commission, and those who lived in the dowdy section of the house with fireplaces crowed over those who lived in the streamlined luxury of our American wing. Yet those who had fireplaces and crowed had all the usual British coughs and colds, while those who lived in the American wing, freezing between their windows and their ventilators, did not raise one cold among them, which seems to indicate that the American way of life is health-promoting, provided it breaks down.

Then the new boiler came, and that is all about the radiators, except that you could get electric shocks off them whenever the house was as much as grazed by lightning.

We lived in a thunderstorm locality, but there was no thunder in the air, there was nothing but a steady downpour of soothing summer rain, on that afternoon when our fire alarm first went into action. Fire drill was promptly carried out, just as in rehearsals. Indeed, everything went off perfectly until it came to finding the fire. In the region indicated by the small flap and the red eye, there was no fire and nothing like one.

The voice of the gong continued its warning note and sounded so exactly like the voice of truth that the search was extended. The house was quite a fair size; there were about seventy rooms in it. My father, my mother, the butler, Mr. Jessop (who had been called in earlier to stop a leak in the scullery), the poodle, and I ran up and down the house, looking everywhere for the fire, while the gong sounded, and the rain beat, and the flood rose steadily in the scullery, and the boys and the servants, standing in their patient, fire-drilled ranks in the road, became increasingly wet and hungry and disillusioned. And then the gonging ceased, and we were left listening to the patter of raindrops and our own exhausted breathing. On the morrow, an expert on fire alarms came down from London and tested ours. It was found to be in perfect working order.

So the next time it went off, we took its word for it. Fire drill was carried out, the fire was systematically sought for — first where it should have been, then everywhere else. Again there was no fire.

This was mortifying, and after our fire alarm's third attempt, which took place at 5 a.m. during a thunderstorm, my father said to the expert, who had again come down from London, tested it, and found nothing wrong with it, that if this sort of thing kept on, he would have the fire alarm taken out and buy a rain gauge, adding, since the expert looked baffled, that a rain gauge does its work modestly, without beating on a tom-tom like an African savage taking part in a rain ceremony.

'Do I understand that your alarm has tended to function in rainy weather?' the expert asked.

'It has so far,' said my father.

The expert gave a sigh of relief and said it must have got wet.

Science is always soothing. When the expert had demonstrated to my father that a drop of rain falling on a sensitive place in the vine would cause a temporary short circuit, and that a short circuit would act just as efficaciously on the mechanism as an outbreak of fire, he took up his hat and his little bag and prepared to go away, like an angel whose task is done. 'It is simply a matter of keeping the apparatus dry,' he said. 'If rain seems likely, it would be advisable to close the windows.'

My mother, who had been pawing the air during this conversation, now said, with simple sarcasm, 'I suppose it never rains in America.' The expert patiently explained that the climate of the United States was calmed and regularized by being a continental climate, and added that the American style of building was better designed for keeping rain out.

That evening, my father announced that the fire alarm's alarms were to be disregarded and that the signal for fire drill would, in future be given by the blowing of whistles. Thereafter, whenever we heard the familiar note of the gong, we just glanced out of the nearest window to see if it was raining. Duly, it always was.

One fine afternoon, some years later, we heard the town fire bell begin to ring, and presently the town fire engine came snorting down the street and drew up outside. It was Mr. Jessop's shed that was on fire. This was next door to our house, an ideal arrangement whenever we had to get hold of Mr. Jessop but not so ideal now, as the shed was full of paintpots and timber and turpentine. There was no disillus-

28

ioned lethargy about this fire drill. The non-combatants filed out as though to the circus, and as soon as I could elude my mother's injunctions about controlling the poodle, I followed them. By now the shed was gloriously alight. Long tongues of fire streaked up our side wall, and one of the hose gangs was told off to keep it sprayed. It was a wonderful experience while it lasted, with steam hissing and paintpots exploding, and my father and the butler leaning out of windows to shout down the latest reports of how hot our wall was getting on the inner side and being extinguished with jets from the hose, and the leader of the fire brigade saying never fear, he would save us yet, and the whistle-blown, fire-drilled ranks of boys standing in the road and enjoying themselves as they had never had an opportunity to do before; and it was not too bad for Mr. Jessop, either, who had been meaning for years to get around to building a new shed and now would have the insurance money to pay for it.

In the end the fire was got under. Everything suddenly became obtrusively wet and dirty. My father and the butler came out reporting that our wall was now nice and cool again, and my father began tipping the hose gang who had looked after it. It was at that moment of relief and felicitation that our fire alarm went off, resounding through the empty house. A last whisk of the hose, lightheartedly spraying the side wall, had gone in through one of the windows and found a sensitive spot on the vine. My father, a man who kept a strong temper under strong control, said in an undertone to the butler, 'Sherwood, go in and put a stop to that thing. Take a hatchet to it, if need be.' And Sherwood, borrowing a hatchet from a fireman, gladly obeyed.

29

My Father, My Mother,
the Bentleys, the Poodle,
Lord Kitchener, and the Mouse

THE first bed, the bed in which I was got and born, was made of brass, with shiny knobs and a starched white valance usually stencilled with dogpaws. By the time I was in my teens it looked shockingly old-fashioned, and my mother decided to replace it by a fourposter, replicated under the influence of Lutyens from some chaste Georgian original. This cost a great deal of money and was made of solid oak. The groans of the men who carried its limbs upstairs and put them together testified to the solidity.

It was because of the uncouthness of the groans, my mother averred, and the powers of association in the canine mind that our poodle concluded that the fourposter was some kind of lofty machine expressly invented for the oppression of poodles, and refused to sleep in the same room with it. Bidden to lie down and be a good dog, he would twitch in a martyred silence till the light was turned off; then he would rise to his feet and begin what my mother, whose childhood was spent in southern India, called Dead-Hindoo-ing. Dead-Hindoo-ing is uttering a succession of those flesh-creeping howls which end in a tremolo. My mother could do it very eloquently herself, and when I was younger had enlarged my mind by telling me how the chief jackal proclaims, 'I've found a dead Hindoo-oo-oo!' to the rest of the pack, who, sitting round on their haunches in the slashing jungle moonlight, bark out, 'Where? Where? Where?' But to have the poodle Dead-Hindoo-ing in nocturnal Middlesex was inappropriate. After several nights of this, the poodle was persuaded to sleep in my father's study, and my mother was able to give her whole mind to enjoying the fourposter.

A few nights later she woke up to hear more animal noises. These were well in keeping with Middlesex, for they came from a mouse. It scampered about the room in a lighthearted, flippant way, pausing at intervals to crunch. Trying to compose herself by the force of Reason, my mother remembered that while she was still striving to rescue the poodle from being a prey to superstition, she had tried biscuits. He must have left some crumbs about, and the mouse had come after them. This was shocking, as it meant that Rose did not really sweep. Rose, on the other hand, darned linen as no housemaid of my mother's had ever darned before; she made her darns adornings. Shaping the diplomatic approach which would indicate the biscuit crumbs without unsettling such a good darner, my mother got over her morbid interest in the mouse, and presently fell asleep again.

The *aide-mémoire* to Rose passed off without mishap, and that night, having ascertained for herself that there were no crumbs, my mother lay down in the fourposter thinking how pleasant it is to fall asleep with a quiet mind. She was still dwelling on the quietness of her mind when she heard the mouse again. This time — umbraged, perhaps, by finding no crumbs — it was in a sterner mood. It approached with a resolute gait and began to gnaw a leg of the bedstead. My mother leaned out of bed and said in an undertone, 'Shoo!' The gnawing ceased, but the mouse did not go away, and presently it began to gnaw again. The rest of the night was spent antiphonally between my mother and the mouse, who formally acknowledged her shooings by brief silences, after which he gnawed on. But by sunrise my mother's voice, strained by the effort of reiterating 'Shoo' in an undertone, was almost exhausted, whereas the mouse, each time it returned to the attack, gnawed more vigorously, as though it were inflamed by rage and defiance.

All through these painful hours, my mother did not think

31

of waking my father. On weekdays he had to get up at quarter to seven, and as he seldom went to bed before midnight, she had strong views about the sacredness of his slumbers. I don't doubt that she would have lain bleeding to death beside him, or racked with the most compelling of sudden thoughts, rather than make a move to waken him. But in the small hours of the following night she prodded him with her elbow and said, 'George! Did you feel the bed shaking just then? Hush. Don't make a sound. It's a mouse.'

As usual, my mother was right. It was a mouse, and it was gnawing. 'There it is!' she exclaimed. 'Did you feel it then? It's shaking the whole bedstead.' No man of intellect cares to base an argument on the obvious. While my father, scorning to assert that a bedstead which four men could only carry with groans could not be shaken by one mouse, was casting about for some more controvertible and interesting disagreement, she continued, 'This has been going on night after night. And always the same leg — the near hind leg. There's nothing else for it — you must fetch Lord Kitchener.'

Lord Kitchener, the only cat I ever knew who chewed his own moustachios, was our respected tabby, and he had become very much of a recluse and spent most of his time in the boiler room. It was from the boiler room that my father carried him, mutely and sullenly resisting, upstairs. 'Mice, Kitchener, mice! Go seek!' cried my mother, who had no real vocation for cats. Lord Kitchener gave her one blighting monosyllabic glance, removed all traces of my father with a few smart licks, and resumed his slumbers. My father watched this with wistful veneration. He, too, would have been glad to resume his slumbers, having washed off some trifling bloodstains and a haunting smell of boiler room. But it was not to be.

'No wonder this house is overrun by mice,' said my mother bitterly. 'Tomorrow I shall go to the Army and Navy and buy a mongoose. But now, as you are up, darling, would you mind fetching the poodle. *He's* not so fat he can't move.'

32

It was not that we had omitted to choose a name for our poodle; we had chosen too many, none of them had stuck, and in the end he was spoken of as the Poodle, just as one says the Pope, or at that date said the Tzar. A willing, romantic animal, he came upstairs enthusiastically prepared to do whatever feats might be expected of him — short of sleeping with that fearful fourposter. On the threshold he cringed. But finding himself propelled into a lighted room where my mother was sitting up in the machine for the oppression of poodles and making encouraging noises, he suddenly developed the valour of the terrified, the acumen of the warrior. There was the cat. This, however wild and unprecedented, was what was expected of him. With a yell, he launched himself on Lord Kitchener. Lord Kitchener scratched his nose with lightning nonchalance and sprang on to the mantelshelf, whence he dislodged several family photographs and Lady Hamilton as a Bacchante. There, if he had not been dragged from his own boiler room, the encounter might have ended, for he was temperamentally a Quietist and asked only for peace with honour. But now, having twice been so rudely disturbed, he needed to shake the black bile off his liver, which he did by rushing round the room at furniture level, scattering destruction as he went, while the poodle bounded in his wake through a hail of pincushions, powder bowls, nail scissors, cardcases, pomade pots, copies of the *Christian Year*, glove stretchers, trinket boxes, small ornaments, cough lozenges, and anything else that Lord Kitchener found available for self-expression.

Roused by the shindy, I was wondering if I would be well received if I joined the family circus when I heard the spare-room door opened, and Mr. and Mrs. Bentley, who were staying with us at the time, consulting together as to what they ought to do. They were a pair of earnest, high-minded numbskulls, so it was only a matter of a few sentences before they knew that they should do their duty. The passage light flicked on. Mr. Bentley, tactfully raising his coughs above the tumult of voices and crashes, crossed the landing and tapped on the bedroom door. As he did so, there was another splintering crash, and the poodle left off baying and began to sneeze.

'Warner, I say, Warner. Is anything wrong?'

Except for the poodle's sneezes, everything had become arrestingly silent, and Mr. Bentley's inquiries must have been plainly audible through the door. But there was no answer. He spoke again, much louder, and rather jerkily. 'I say, Warner! Is there anything wrong?'

My father, speaking as though he had a clothespeg on his nose, answered in what would have seemed untroubled tones except for the effect of the clothespeg. 'Thank you, thank you. There's nothing wrong. We had to intimidate a mouse, that was all. I'm sorry if we disturbed you.'

Mr. Bentley said, 'Not at all,' sneezed, and went back to Mrs. Bentley.

A minute later, the bedroom door was opened from within, and Lord Kitchener and the poodle came out, walking soberly side by side in an odour of aromatic ammonia — for the last victim of Lord Kitchener's self-expression had been my mother's bottle of strong smelling salts.

When the Bentleys came down to breakfast, it was plain that they had agreed to draw a veil. It was also plain that my mother had been made aware of the graces of contrition.

'Coffee or tea? Thank God they both seem pretty strong. I'm sure we all need it after such an appalling night.'

Parrying this implication that both Bentleys had been sleeping in my parents' bedroom, Mrs. Bentley said that she and Eustace preferred tea — and took it weak.

'I'd hate you to think that I'd make such a fuss about any normal mouse,' my mother said. 'But this one has been persecuting me for ages, and last night it came to a head.'

'A mouse?' Mrs. Bentley spoke as if she belonged to some cool, calm world into which mice never climbed.

'It ground its teeth like a sawmill. I wonder you didn't hear it.'

34

'No.'

'Really,' my mother said, as though speaking from some world into which no Ginevra Bentley with her adenoids would ever climb, and turned to Mr. Bentley. 'You heard it, though. At least, you heard something, for you came to our help. It was very kind of you.'

'I heard the dog barking. It struck me that your room might be on fire. That's all. One reads of such things.'

'Yes, doesn't one? Dear angels! And whole slum families saved, poor wretches! — though one sometimes wonders what for.'

My father, seeing that Mrs. Bentley was about to burst out of her ice cavern, remarked that this angel was barking at the cat, and that he was very sorry the Bentleys should have been disturbed.

Mr. Bentley, scrupulously just, said that my mother had been disturbed, too. Mice could be quite disturbing.

My mother suddenly looked very happy. 'Of course! Now I understand why it upset me. It was gnawing the leg of the bed, and at the back of my mind I must have thought it was that Indian mouse. You know — it gnaws the root of the tree which holds up the world. I expect our butler, Ragaloo, told me, He knew a lot of stories.'

'The tree Ygdrasil,' said Mrs. Bentley. 'But isn't it in Scandinavian mythology? And isn't the mouse an adder?'

'Sanskrit first,' said my mother. 'And a mouse. Indians know too much about snakes to suppose they gnaw. They'd ruin their poison fangs. I can remember my ayah finding a clutch of cobra's eggs in a broken wall, and how she took a stone and smashed each egg — squashed them, really. The eggs are soft, like kid gloves. Then she picked me up and ran full tilt down a hillside covered with small dahlias, in case the mother cobra should come after us. That must have been in the Shevaroy Hills, where I saw gold fern and silver fern.' She looked at the Bentleys as serenely as if they were not there, though in fact it was she who had gone away, carried off face downward under a never failing bangled arm.

35

My mother's recollections of her childhood in India were so vivid to her that they became inseparably part of my own childhood, like the arabesques of a wallpaper showing through a coating of distemper. It was I who saw the baby cobras writhing as the stone hammered the flaccid eggs. It was to me that the man fishing in the Adyar River gave the little pink-and-yellow fish which I afterwards laid away among my mother's nightdresses, alone in a darkened room under a swaying punkah. It was I who made sweet-scented necklaces by threading horsehair through the tamarind blossoms which fell on the garden's watered lawn. I was there when the ceiling cloth broke and pink baby rats dropped on the dining-room table; when the gardener held up the dead snake at arm's stretch and still there was a length of snake dragging on the ground; when the scorpion bit the ayah. It was my bearer who led me on my pony through a tangle of narrow streets, and held me up so that I saw through a latticed window a boy child and a girl child, swathed in tinsel and embroideries and with marigold wreaths round their necks, sitting cross-legged on the ground among small dishes of sweetmeats, and who then made me promise never to tell my parents—which I never did. It was I whom the bandicoot visited in my night nursery, nosing in my palm for titbits—another thing which I kept to myself, bandicoots having a bad name among elders and servants. It was I, wearing a wreath of artificial forget-me-nots, who drove to St. George's Cathedral to be a bridesmaid, with an earthenware jar in the carriage, from which water was continually ladled out and poured over my head; for this being an English wedding it had to take place in the worst heat of the day. It was I, though I blushed for it, who, coming back past the jail from my early-morning rides, used to put out my tongue at the prisoners. It was I whom the twirling masoola boat carried through the surf to the P. & O. liner, on that first stage of a journey towards an unknown land which was called home.

The harshness of an English winter and of an English nurse disabled my mother like a mortal sickness, snapping the continuity between the adored precocious child in Madras and the stupefied little malapert in Hampshire — whose skin was yellow, whose legs were spindleshanks, who could not even repeat the alphabet, because she was one of those unfortunate Indian children. What was the use of remembering everything when you could recall nothing? Only when she had a child of her own, a confidante and a contemporary, was she able to repossess herself. Then she began to unpack this astonishing storehouse, full of scents and terrors, flowers, tempests, monkeys, beggars winding worms out of their feet, a couple of inches a day, not more, or the worm broke and you had to begin again, undislodgeable holy men who came and sat in the garden, the water carrier's song — and as she talked as much for her own pleasure as mine, and made no attempts to be instructive or consecutive, I never tired of listening. I remember being rather puzzled why we never went to India, since we often went to London; the journey to London took less than an hour, and India would have been more interesting.

Another misconception lasted longer. Though I don't recollect how it came out that for years I had supposed that the groom in the photograph of my grandfather's charger was my grandfather himself, I remember her plain, factual correction: 'Your grandfather had a white skin and was a much smaller man.'

Interval for Metaphysics

THERE is a period in one's life — perhaps not longer than six months — when one lives in two worlds at once, floating like thistledown from the bosom of Aristotle to the bosom of Plato, and effortlessly resolving the debate between the Realists and the Nominalists. It is the time when one has freshly learned to read. The Word, till then a denominating aspect of the Thing, has suddenly become detached from it and is perceived as a glittering entity, transparent and unseizable as a jellyfish, yet able to create an independent world that is both more recondite and more instantaneously convincing than the world one knew before. In that first world, a star, for instance, is always attached — to the night sky, to the top of the Christmas Tree, to the bosom of a lady's dress; but at the moment one is able to create the star out of those four letters, it is set free, and develops an attaching gravity of its own, gathering to itself poles, garters, and the smell of an evening paper.

But there are also occasions when the word, exploding on the surface of the thing, remains there, coruscating like a nova. There was a chemist in our town called P. St. John Gunn. To enter his shop filled me with an invariable solemn joy, such as is afforded to some by entering a church, or to others by entering a wine cellar. Like a church, it was dusky, and the light of outer day, striking through the three flasks in the window, cast stained-glass glories of crimson, orange-tawny, and amethyst. But it was more reticent than a church, for its wares, instead of being displayed, were hidden away in cabinets of countless little drawers, in cylindrical black glass jars lettered with gold, or in brown pottery canisters. I seldom visited this holy place. My mother did not believe in medicines. But it was joy enough to gaze on its exterior, which had a sombre lustrous magnificence, a pomp of gold and sable, such as I never saw equalled till I saw a hearse in Rome. Black glass, sleek as the jars within, and ornamented with gold scrollings and curlicues, screened the lower two-thirds of the window. Above, on a hanging shelf, stood the three flasks, vouchsafing only the barest hint of the colours they were lavishing on wall and floor within. Above again was the nameboard, and this, too, was of black glass, and its gold letters had bevelled edges, so that they seemed to be coated in radiance. It was on this nameboard, which, after one of those rare visits to the shop, I had looked back to admire, that the name of P. St. John Gunn suddenly exploded in evangelical majesty. Undoubtedly, I thought, a descendant. A slipshod method of speech had obscured the glorious name, but the letter revealed it. So on my return I told my mother that Nannie had bought a new sponge from Saint John Gunn. My mother corrected my pronunciation. She was infallible, but the revelation was infallible, too, so the four Evangelists became Saint Matthew, Saint Mark, Saint Luke, and Sinjohn.

My mother was infallible. My father made no such claim, but he had a fine assortment of irrefutable doubts. Among other things, he doubted — and very naturally, I'm sure, being a schoolmaster — the benefit of learning to read. From the moment a child discovers that information can be got out of books, he averred, it desists from exercising its faculties of observation, memory, and thinking for itself. So, long after my contemporaries had become literate, I was left to be observant, retentive, and rational. When my formal education began, with an illustrated spelling book, my faculties of observation, etc., prompted me to glance at the picture before saying that the Ox was Fat, the Ap-ple Ro-sy; and I was thought a promising scholar till the day when I maintained that NAG spelled 'horse,' or at least 'pony.' My mother then decided that I should learn my

reading from the Bible. Its stories would interest me, and
the noble English of the King James Version would improve
my vocabulary. I don't know whether she thought the
English of the Old Testament was nobler or its stories more
suitable for a child, or whether it was just her tidy mind that
liked to begin at the beginning. Anyhow, I began at the
beginning, reading aloud, with a pause at the end of each
verse to get my strength up, and with my mother's comments to encourage me on. I, reading: 'And they heard the
voice of the Lord God walking in the garden —' My mother,
in a vehement undertone: 'Sneak!' These moral judgments
(when we came on to the Patriarchs, she could bring herself
to approve only of Noah, because he made room for the
animals — God's idea, really, but Him she was prejudiced
against almost from the start — and Esau, because he was
not Jacob) helped me along what was a rather craggy path,
and insensibly prepared me for the lesson of 'La Comédie
Humaine': that odious characters have a heaven appointed
for them in great literature. As for my vocabulary, it
became so episcopal and enlarged that it had to be explained to me that though the language of the Bible was part
of the national heritage it was not to be used in public. Obviously, such a prohibition could not hold against what was
said aloud in church. So when our fat old spaniel trotted into the butcher's shop and scavenged a gobbet out of the
scrap bucket, it was with a clear conscience and a sense of
saying the right thing that I exclaimed, as I dragged him
away, 'Friday! Thou shalt not commit adultery!' Yet it was
all wrong, somehow. The butcher averted his face and my
nurse looked furious and took me straight home. Flouncing
in on my mother, she said she had borne much but could
bear no more, and wished to give notice. When I was asked
to explain myself, I took my stand, rather aggrievedly, on
reason. Had I not asked my mother what adultery meant?
Had she not explained that it was the sins of the flesh? I
could not understand why there should be all this fuss.

Reason was allowed to prevail. But I suppose my mother
felt that my language had been sufficiently ennobled, for

40

the Bible was laid aside and I began to do sums. My arithmetic has since given far more cause for public affront and affright, but this could scarcely have been foreseen at the time.

Anyhow, I still think that Florence and the butcher were straining at gnats. What was my trifling departure from the normal compared to the eccentricities permanently on show in our small community of hard-working schoolmasters and their highminded wives? I was no odder than Mr. Lancelot, who was regularly to be observed leaning out of an upper window in his nightshirt, apparently in rather breathless communion with the stilly night but at intervals exclaiming in measured utterance, 'Bi, Ba, Bo!'—the fact being that he was so busy all day that only then could he find time to attend to his lungs, which were weak and needed the exercise of deep breathing, and to his elocution, which he was studying to improve. I was no odder than Mr. Tennyson, who went about soliloquizing in deaf-and-dumb language. I was no odder than Mr. Vaughan, who memorized his sermons by repeating them to his goat, or Mrs. Vaughan, who drove herself furiously in a wheelchair fitted with a mechanical cuckoo. I was no odder than Mr. Southey, who distracted the fishmonger by demanding lampreys. I was not odder than Mrs. MacArthur's ermine tippet.

My mother surveyed such antics with a rather *de-haut-en-bas* appreciation; for she saw herself as a counter-exponent of the regular, the conventional, the ordinary—resolved on behaving like other people, though she were the only person to behave so. This lent a magistral quality to her own eccentricities, just as her obedience to the latest rulings of fashion about hats made her successive hats so meteorically outstanding. She gave a like obedience to a code of proper deportment. These rulings were invariable: with your superiors, be calm and simple; with your equals, be pleasant without overdoing it; with your inferiors, be all that is cordial and amiable. It is an excellent code, and no one could have said a word against her adherence to it if it had not been for Bottles. Bottles was a local rascal, a cor-

41

pulent, crimson rascal, with a game leg and a moist alcoholic eye, who carried a few bootlaces about with him on the pretext of vending them. My mother, out walking, would meet an acquaintance, and pause to be pleasant without overdoing it. Bottles would spy her, and shout out from the farther side of the street, 'And how's my little sweetheart this morning?' At Bottles' calm and simple address, my mother would break off whatever she was saying, and reply with 'Bottles, come here! I want to talk to you about your boots.' Bottles would lumber up, simpering affectionately, to be assured that if he went on pawning my father's erstwhile boots instead of wearing them he would die of bronchitis. So would he please redeem them and set her mind at rest? Meanwhile the acquaintance stood there enduring Bottles' breath, or, more probably, slid away. My mother had sundry other rascals, but Bottles was her dearest. He had a good heart, he was always so nice to Friday, and the colouring of his nose, a rich mottle of crimson and purple, was a joy to her artistic eye. One day she got him, fleas and all, into the house, gave him a composing draught, sat him down, and painted his portrait. It was a good portrait, but the nose, she said, was too cold in tone. She had put too much blue into it. This indeed was so. She had put her finger on it, as usual. She was infallible — or almost infallible. 'It's an extraordinary thing,' she remarked, quitting a perambulator over which she and a friend had been stooping with polite congratulations. 'That baby's not in the least like Mr. Liddon.' After a silent wrestle with my mother's influence, the friend replied, 'But why should it be?'

Yet at the time, as I can still manage to remember, it was not as I describe it. Nothing was odd, nothing was amusing. Children do not recognize oddity — their pride, on which they depend for their footing in the world, forbids it — and they are amused only by jokes and horseplay. Mr. Tennyson went by, constructing and brushing away his inaudible words as though accompanied by a swarm of invisible wasps. Mrs. Vaughan swept around the corner, sounding

42

her cuckoo. Bottles sat breathing heavily beneath the Arun-
del print of 'St. Jerome in His Study'. There they were; interesting, of course, for everything was interesting; but not
remarkable. But my whole soul hung on the chance of
seeing that girl in her teens who had a club foot, and was
dressed in black, and carried an oblong dressbox wrapped
in black oilcloth. She fascinated me. I watched for her out
of the window, I listened for her stumping tread. There was
no discoloration of pity or terror in my thoughts. She
fascinated me because I did not know the words for her, and
at the same time knew that such words were her due, and
waited, intently trembling, till they should explode into life
and clothe her, as the bevelled edges appeared to coat the
name of P. St. John Gunn in radiance—that sad little
dressmaker's apprentice, sent to and fro on errands or to
deliver what was in the dressbox.

For to that extent I was quite aware of the difference between the bosom of Aristotle and the bosom of Plato,
however rapid and effortless the journey between them.
There was a world of things, in which everything had its
name and place, and there was a world of words, in which
everything came to life. Each was valid, and there was no
call to choose between them, for both were mine. Thus, it
was possible to stand looking at a wooden paling and
hearing Mr. Vaughan behind it, saying in his quavering old
tenor voice, 'Let us ta-ake Saint Fra-ancis,' and the goat
saying, 'Ba-a-a!,' and at the same moment be listening to
the music of the spheres, because the word 'paling' had suddenly developed its attaching gravity, and had gathered to
itself the pale primrose that forsaken dies, and a certain expression that the sky puts on at dusk, and that I had rarely
seen, since I was supposed to be indoors by then.

I was also supposed not to dawdle but to go briskly on my
afternoon walks, to bowl my hoop or twirl my skipping
rope. 'Come on, child, hurry up! Don't moon so.' *Moon* . . .
a round honey-coloured state, and at the same time a spiky
ornament, in Florence's Aristotelian vocabulary. Though
the two worlds did not enforce a choice on me, I knew they

43

were distinct, and even opposed; for otherwise, how should things, at the breath of a word, be loosened from their *de-facto* irrevocability and become subjects for speculation, comparison, doubt, and inquiry, so that one could say 'Why?' and utter that noble human sentence 'I don't believe it.'

And afterwards, as if angered, the world of things reasserts itself, and one is the prey of ambition and covet, and wants admiration, and bronze dancing slippers, and an iron hoop instead of a wooden one. The word sinks back into the thing, or at best betakes itself to the printed page. The period when one lived in two worlds at once is over. *Perhaps not longer than six months,* I said. When I try to recall it, I cannot retain it for as many minutes.

Fried Eggs are Mediterranean

M Y father was a schoolmaster — a rather naysaying profession. In private life, he redressed the balance by falling in with my mother's wishes whenever this did not lead directly to crime or public riot. So when she wanted a holiday cottage in Devonshire which should be weather-proof, vicar-proof — in other words, so discouragingly sequestered that only tradesmen's vans would think it worth their while to approach it — with masses of hydrangeas, sheets of gentians, and rational cupboards, he bought a small rocky meadow under a shoulder of the moor, found a steady architect, and told him to build a cottage in accordance with my mother's notions. All this concern about gentians, cupboards, and inaccessibility was ancillary to my mother's prime notion — to explore the ravishing novelty of doing without any servants. Even in that distant golden age there was talk about the Simple Life, and similar aspirations were expressed by other ladies with their proper complements of cooks, housemaids, butlers, and so forth; but for the most part wistfully, as they also expressed a desire to live on a South Sea island. My mother's aspirations had more bottom to them. At one time in her girlhood, she had somehow penetrated into a kitchen and brought away the conviction that cooking is the most succulent of human pleasures. There, too, she had discovered that the food you eat out of its saucepan tastes infinitely better than ever it does by the time it has been conveyed to a dining-room and withered under a conversational host. So the architect was told to make an L-shaped kitchen. The leg of the L was the kitchen proper, with a back door opening from it, so that if you wanted more coal or a bay leaf, you could get it without waste of time; the remainder was what we should now call a dining-alcove — though it was about three times as large as any dining-alcove of now, with a bow window, a couple of dining-room portraits, and a whole series of its own peculiar draughts.

The draughts manifested themselves immediately, for our initial visit took place in an Easter holiday, when all that you could see of the beauties of Devonshire was gigantic primroses looming through sheets of driving rain. And how odious it would have been, my mother said, if we had brought any servants — all catching colds, yearning for town diversions, and giving notice. As for the draughts, they would go away as soon as the chimneys had warmed up, and meanwhile our food would be so deliciously hot that we should never give a thought to them. We were a party of five — my father, my mother, our poodle, myself — at that time with my hair still down my back and conspicuously less well-groomed than the poodle's — and one of my father's young men. My father's young men were part of our family landscape. No sooner had his pupils gone on to a university than they were irresistibly drawn to come back on visits — to snatch the fearful joy of addressing him as Warner instead of calling him Sir, my mother opined, but also, perhaps, because they were more attached to him than they could realize while they were under his rod and staff. This particular young man was called Philip. During our first day in the cottage, he and my father were given over to dynamite, blasting holes for gentians to grow in, while my mother and I arranged the larder and calmed the poodle. As for our meals, they came, tranquil and luxurious, out of a hamper. Cooking would begin on the morrow, said my mother. Breakfast would be porridge with Devonshire cream, followed by boiled eggs. The reason she adduced for this menu was that she would be too busy for anything really ambitious. The real reason, however, was on the kitchen dresser, in the form of a small hourglass whose sands would run just so long as it took to boil an egg. This object had aroused her strongest passions, and for months she had been longing to use it.

The porridge would have been wholly successful if it had not been for the unamalgamability of the Devonshire cream. We did our best to be pleased, however, and looked forward to the eggs. No eggs could have looked more promising than they did, quite dwarfing the eggcups, but they were so under-cooked as to be uneatable. 'I can't understand it,' said my mother. 'I never took my eye off the hourglass.' My father muttered something about *la mystique*. Philip, a courteous guest, daresayed that the hourglass was timed to town eggs—puny specimens. I remarked that there was still some cold tongue, and the poodle looked intensely agreeing. But my mother was not going to be beaten at the starting post. She fastened on Philip's suggestion; naturally, Devonshire eggs being so much larger and fresher than town eggs, they would take longer to boil. She would try again, and this time she would run the hourglass twice. She did so. We ate toast, and watched the sands running through, and it seemed a long time to wait for a boiled egg. These eggs came out like hot marble, but we said they were delicious, and ate them before my mother could take them away.

Lunch and dinner were triumphs of cookery; so were the grilled sausages next morning. But it was obvious that the business of the boiled eggs was preying on my mother's mind. She was too proud not to admit a failure, but she deeply disliked failing. On her next essay, she decided to time the eggs by her watch, four minutes exactly. Unfortunately, our poodle as a puppy had been terrified by a life-size advertisement for cod-liver oil, and when the postman came in wearing waders (it was, of course, still raining) the poodle thought the deep-sea diver had got off the hoarding and come for him. In the flurry that ensued, my mother's attention was diverted. She lost her count of time and thought the flurry had taken longer than it really had. The eggs were snatched from the pot, and were undercooked.

47

That afternoon, my father and Philip went out fishing. River trout would be very nice for breakfast, and might distract my mother from brooding on eggs. So they thought, though my father should have known my mother's undistractible mind, once she had got her teeth into anything. She professed herself delighted with the trout, but qualified this by asking who on earth would clean them. My father said he would clean them; and after exclaiming, 'Poor little things!' and stipulating that the cleaning should be done out of doors, she appeared to give way. But by the morning she had decided that there is not much staying power in a trout, so the trout would be followed by boiled eggs; and this time she would make sure that the water was performing what the cookery book called 'a full rolling boil' before the eggs were dropped in. The trout having been eaten as a species of hors d'oeuvres, my mother secluded herself in a cloud of steam, we glued out attention on our watches, and for four minutes nothing was heard except a tumult of boiling. But whether these four anxious minutes were enough could not be decided, because the water had boiled so rollingly that all the shells had cracked, and the eggs had been transmogrified into a sort of depraved froth and some pellets.

As though her mind had switched to higher things, my mother said dreamily, 'Do you think we've got a prayer book? I know we've got dozens at home, but is there one here?'

My father thought not, and asked what she wanted it for.

'Oh, just the Fifty-first Psalm.'

'We've got a Bible,' he said. 'The prayer-book translation is earlier than the Bible version. Would that matter?'

My mother considered. 'I don't think so. At any rate, let's try it!'

When my father came back with a Bible, he inquired with controlled curiosity, 'Nora, what are we going to try the Fifty-first Psalm for?'

'Boiling the next lot of eggs by. I remembered last night, when I was thinking about it, that I had read in some old

48

miscellany book or other that in the days before watches, when people had only those worthless hourglasses to depend on, they used a psalm for boiling eggs—but I couldn't remember which. Now I've remembered. It was the Fifty-first, for I thought at the time, what a gloomy proceeding.'

I remembered reading something of this sort, too, and said so.

'Am I to read it aloud?' said my father, having found the place with dexterity, 'or must I intone it?'

'Neither. I shall read myself. You'd make it too majestic, for we've only got middle-sized eggs left. You can put them in, and say "Go." And then you must stand there, ready to take them out the moment I say "Amen." '

My father handed over the Bible, put the eggs in, and said 'Go.' My mother replied with 'Have mercy upon me, O God, according to Thy loving kindness: according unto the multitude of Thy tender mercies blot out my transgressions. Wash me thoroughly from mine iniquity, and cleanse me from my sin. For I acknowledge my transgressions: and my sin is ever before me . . .' She was overhauling the seventh verse when there came a knock on the back door. Saying in a rapid parenthesis, 'They're all we have left,' my mother went on reading, and after another knock the postman opened the door. Philip fell on his knees. I followed Philip's example. Without comment the postman put down some parcels and went away, shutting the door unobtrusively. The eggs were the best we'd achieved, but even so they were a trifle overcooked.

'I'm sure he thought it was family prayers,' said my mother. 'Philip showed great presence of mind. For we don't want the postman thinking that we are maniacs; he's unpunctual enough as it is.'

'He might think it a little odd that we had eaten fish first,' objected my father.

'Not in Lent.'

Though Philip was now addressing my father as Warner as a mere matter of course, he must have kept some vestiges of piety and awe, for he shot a glance of staggered ad-

49

miration towards my mother. She saw it. She always saw such glances. But she misunderstood it, and thought he was admiring her as a cook, not as a casuist. 'They're not perfect yet,' she said with modest pride.

'Not quite, perhaps,' said Philip. 'But now I've got a slight theory about it. I believe that the psalm should be read in Latin. These traditional customs go a long way back; they were part of medieval culture, and medieval culture was mainly monastic. If a monk were boiling eggs (and we know that they ate them either boiled or poached; fried eggs for some reason are Mediterranean), he would time them in Latin. Or so it seems to me. At any rate, I do think we ought to experiment. These things are so intensely interesting. So unless there is anything more important that I can do, I shall go into Exeter and buy a Vulgate.'

Timed by the Vulgate, the eggs came out just as they should, and we went on boiling them in Latin until my mother found that she knew by nature when they were ready. By then, I had remembered which old miscellany book contained this precious advice, and had looked it up. The time prescribed was 'no longer than whiles you can say the Miserere Psalm very leisurely.' The extract was headed, 'How Long to Infuse Tea. Sir Kenelm Digby's Method.'

The Gorgeous West

MY mother was not a woman to blench at novelties. I do not claim that she embodied a spirit of dauntless research into the unknown, but if she heard or read of anything new she didn't want to be behindhand in getting hold of it. Accordingly, one morning in the first decade of this century our breakfast table displayed a bowl of yellow fruit — globular, like oranges, but larger and sleeker. 'Grapefruit,' she said, in the casual manner she reserved for such introductions. 'Americans eat them. At breakfast.'

'How?' asked my father.

She knew that too. 'With spoons. Cut in half and sugared.'

But she was not prepared for the resistance of that sleek rind, nor for the quantity of pips and the toughness of segmental fibre we encountered after sawing our way in. 'Scissors,' she presently remarked. 'Sylvia, run upstairs to my room and bring down the pair of sharp-nosed scissors from the workbox on the windowsill. Not my embroidery scissors, nor the scissors I cut out with. The plain strong scissors I do odd jobs with.'

The plain strong scissors looked too workaday to be appropriate to this interesting novelty; but they got over the difficulty of the segmental fibres and left us with only the pips to contend with. (Science does good as well as harm: the grapefruit of that date were paved with pips.)

All this took some time and I, at any rate, got incommodiously sticky. Relaxing with grilled kidneys, my father observed that grapefruit was probably a regional breakfast dish eaten by leisured persons in the Southern

51

States. And prepared for them, I added, by slaves. But our little revolt went for nothing. Grapefruit had got on to our breakfast table.

I have lived for a long time. In one respect I date from the Tudors. Our breakfasts were literal: we broke our fast on them. The school bell rang at six-forty-five. Half an hour later my father was giving his first lesson. This venerable schedule was part of the school tradition, and considered by some maniacs on the staff (he was not among them) as being peculiarly conducive to health and right feeling. One of the maniacs had written a school song about it, which began

> Awake, boys, awake!
> The joys of the morning take,

stressed early rising as part of the natural order, and dwelt on the example set by the lesser forms of creation.

> And delicate things on feet and wings
> Are busily finding work to do.

(There was no winter in that gentleman's year.)

Meanwhile, less delicate things were also busy. Servants were cooking, sweeping, bedmaking. My mother would have put in a spell of answering letters, paying bills, and going round the house and garden to see what was wrong with them. I would have combed the poodle and pranced through those 'Études de la Vélocité' I was on prancing terms with. By the time we met at breakfast we wanted something more immediate than grapefruit. They persisted; but later persisted as an alternative to porridge and eventually drifted into the region of dessert and you could have one at the end if you felt like it.

When we had visitors the grapefruit resumed their position as creditable novelties, and held it till the morning some sort of cousin told us he used to breakfast on them constantly when he lived, I've forgotten precisely where but somewhere in the neighbourhood of the Euphrates; at which my mother with an unexpected volte-face said that of course she'd far rather have a mango. The sort of cousin went on to tell us that the real name for them was shaddock, and that some Biblical scholars believed that the apple for which Adam doomed the human race was in fact a shaddock. Convinced, as are all faithful members of the Church of England, that Adam fell for a Cox's Orange Pippin, we pooh-poohed this.

Not long after, my mother tired of grapefruit and introduced a novelty from New England — cod steaks fried in a coating of oatmeal. A stern glamour coated the cod steaks, like the oatmeal: the Pilgrim Fathers, the New England conscience, Boston, hellfire, sassafras (whatever that might be), long winters, long sermons, skunk cabbage, *The Scarlet Letter*, and so on. But it is not in the nature of cod to be a novelty for long, and we went back to kippers.

After that, we ceased to hold the gorgeous West in fee until my father discovered popcorn balls.

He brought them back from London, where duty had cornered him into attending a conference on education. They had caught his eye in a confectioner's window, he explained — dangling from one finger a large white box, tied up so splendidly in quantities of red ribbon and ornamental bows that it had the air of coming from a Parisian milliner who was experimenting with a new variety of midinette. Inside the box, nestling in fortifications of tissue paper, were four wax-paper bags. Inside each bag was a rugged spherical object, one pink, one blue, one yellow, and one a depraved mauve. It was not surprising they had caught his eye.

'How am I supposed to eat these?' my mother asked. 'You can't expect me to bite them. I am not a crocodile.'

It was scarcely the spirit of dauntless research into the unknown. Other people's novelties had to be viewed with discrimination — and when I remember some of mine I agree.

'Try two forks,' said my father. 'Pin it down with one and attack it with the other.'

Even when attacked with forks, the popcorn balls were

not easy to subdue. They were very honestly constructed; the icing sugar that held the puffed maize kernels together extended into every crevice. Force could do nothing much against such steadfastness. My mother tried it, and the bit she dislodged fastened on the poodle, who lay down and rolled on it. 'God knows why we're eating this,' she said, and reverted to fingers. It was obviously a fight to the death, so I followed her example. Only my father, fastidiously pecking on with his forks, remained relatively unadhesive, and calm enough to diagnose flavours assorted to colourings. 'Rose,' he pronounced, sampling our demolitions, 'violet, orange flower —' My mother unclenched her jaws and said, 'And I suppose the blue one is *forget-me-not*.' He said politely she might be right and, obligingly, that he would go up to London to buy some more so as to be sure of it. And he did so.

My mother laughed at his infatuation. I took it more seriously, and brooded. I admired my father for his intellect, I loved him for his character, and till now I had believed in his taste. How could he, then, stoop to that pink, that yellow, that mawkish blue, that quite appalling mauve? It distressed me to blush for him, but blush I did.

I was grown up, and he untimely dead, and the pleasure of being in Paris had put him out of my mind when a hawker of lascivious pictures paused on the terrace of a café in Montparnasse. '*Les poupoules,*' he chanted, '*les belles poupoules.*'

All was explained. I was not the only one to love my father for his character. He had an uncontrollable charm for respectable middle-aged women. It was his cross, and he bore it. But there was a seraglio side to him, as there is to every proper man, and those rounded, pastel-coloured sweetmeats had appealed to it.

The Cheese

I THINK with envy of the children of Rome. What children want from a picture is plain statement enriched by gaudiness. They admire a demonstrably clever and neat-fingered technique, with no art concealing art about it. Whether or no the picture tells a story is immaterial to them since they make up their own stories. The children of Rome have only to walk into Santa Prassede, Santa Maria Maggiore, St. John Lateran — or for that matter many admirable fish restaurants — to find just what they want in the mosaics. By the time I walked into these establishments considerations of art and history had clouded my vision. I was admiring what I ought to admire and saying what I should say: in the churches, 'The design is so majestic, so unequivocal'; in the restaurants, 'It's extraordinary how the tradition hangs on.' But somewhere inside my grown-up self I was aware of a child's beady-eyed expectation at last and fulfillingly satisfied; when I was the right age for pictorial mosaic there was only the Cheese.

However, I got a great deal of pleasure out of the Cheese.

No one directed me to the Cheese. I might not have found it, if my nurse had not been on such conversational terms with the nurse at the Rectory, whom she looked in on just for a minute or two from time to time. While the minutes extended and multiplied I was left to entertain myself in the churchyard. It was a fine crowded churchyard, democratic, too, with all sorts and conditions; parishioners lying higgledy-piggledy under two centuries' taste in monumental masonry: crosses, headstones, altar and coffer tombs, Victorian broken pillars with carved ivy climbing up them, earlier pillars without, cherubs, some grieving, some taking a brighter view, urns, obelisks, reclining anchors — in short, a variety of tombstones in various degrees of preservation (a slab in one altar tomb had a challenging crack across it) as well as many little grassy hillocks with jam pots and seasonal bouquets. There was also Port, a guard on the London & North-Western Railway, whose epitaph my nurse would read aloud, with an appreciative 'Poor fellow!' as an Amen.

> Bright rose the Morn and with it rose poor Port.
> Gay on the Train he used his wonted sport.
> When Evening came to close the fatal Day
> A mutilated Corpse the Sufferer lay.

Since children make up their own stories, I knew that Port spent the intervals between one station and another by frisking along the running board and exclaiming 'Peep-Bo!' to passengers; but by inadvertence fell off and was run over.

Farther on, and standing aristocratically apart with an iron railing enclosing it, was a structure like a sombre summerhouse — a summerhouse designed to be used in very wet weather by people who because of the weather had given up all interest in an outer world. It was windowless, except for a four-inch glazed slit in the rear wall. Its peaked roof had guttering under the eaves, though nothing so worldly as a water butt. Between it and the railings was a narrow paved walk, where dead leaves accumulated. The ground sloped away in front of it, and this, together with the peaked roof, allowed the architect an extra couple of feet in the height of his western façade. Here, behind a padlocked gate in the railing, was a defensively conceived door with iron hinge-bars crossing it, and iron studs set close between them. Centred above the door was the Cheese — a round plaque of mosaic embedded in the wall.

It was a half Stilton which had been allowed to fall into very bad repair. Mice had gnawed holes in it, tunnelling into its verdigris interior; much of its base had been eaten away. I have never seen a minuter or more exact mosaic.

56

Every rent was there, every wrinkle and fissure, every discoloration. Yet it still retained an air of massiveness and
dignity. You could see that in better days, when a clean
napkin was wrapped round it and a silver cheese scoop cir-
cumspectly delved in it, it had been a fine cheese. For some
queer reason — perspective, perhaps — the artist, for all his
technical mastery, had shirked giving it a plate to stand on.
The Cheese was, as it were, suspended against a cornflower-
blue disc — which didn't do as well. But the disc was a
beautiful shade of blue, even if it couldn't be a plate, and
showed off to perfection the rich melancholy mottle of the
Cheese itself — the browns and dusty beiges and bleached
greys brightening to the raw yellow of London clay,
declining to lichenous tints of mildew. I knew every detail of
it, and knew that when I saw it again every detail would be
reliably there. This was a great part of its charm for me.
The mosaic imperturbability absolved me from the human
responsibility to be responsive or grateful or polite. The
Cheese remained in its being and I remained in mine. But
once, on a stormy autumnal afternoon, when a shaft of sun-
light broke through the clouds, I felt the Cheese and the
sunset and the falling leaves and the smell of the bonfire in
the Rectory garden and the wetness of my shoes in the
churchyard grass as a single perception, as though they
were held together by some mysterious glue.

Naturally, I never spoke about the Cheese. It posed no
questions, since it was so indubitably a cheese; and I did not
want anybody else coming to admire it. I had asked my
nurse about the summerhouse. She told me it was a
Maw-soleum, and that no one could get into it now as the
family it belonged to were all dead or gone abroad. I had
no wish to get into it. I pouched the word, and left it at that.
The Cheese was there, wherever the family might be.

I suppose a child with more religion would have known
from the start that the Cheese was a skull. But I was unused
to skulls, except on pirates' flags and corroborated with
crossbones, whereas my father's Stiltons were a venerated
part of our home life. How and when I lost this illusion I

can't remember. It is nothing to children to lose their illusions, tadpoles are much more put about when they lose their tails.

Scenes of Childhood

SPACE is subject to time. The garden I recall was an oblong, twenty by fifteen yards, perhaps; the garden I remember was more than twice as long as the morning shadow of the almond tree and as wide as America; it contained a sweetbriar, a city of reversed flowerpots, a central prairie where bird food was scattered in winter, a Gloire de Dijon rose, a rubbish heap, two paths, and a group of white lilies, where I had to stand on tiptoe in order to get my nose adjusted to the heart of the scent and smudged with pollen.

There was a dark path and a light path. Along the light path ran a low dividing fence, and beyond the fence was the neighbouring garden and Mr. Scudamore. I suppose the neighbouring garden was the same size as ours, since the houses were identical; but it seemed commandingly larger because Mr. Scudamore gardened so earnestly and kept down the weeds and tied up annuals and always called flowers by their botanical names. Our cat visited his garden pretty regularly—cats prefer a nice clean tilth to scratch in—and when circumstances compelled, Mr. Scudamore and my father would converse without bitterness across the fence. The rubbish heap was at the end of the dark path, which began as a narrow arched passageway where the dustbins stood, continued on under a high containing wall, and was shadowed by a row of black poplars growing at a higher level in the builder's yard beyond. Horseradish grew here in morbid profusion, but not much else.

It was on the rubbish heap that I transcended existence.

59

It was higher than usual, augmented by the garden debris of late summer. A bundle of old peasticks had been thrown there. I climbed it, and trod on the peasticks, and heard them snap under my feet, and felt the rubbish heap sidling as I moved. I stared at the wall, and the poplar trees rustled, and the rubbish heap became a raft, and the ocean where it floated directionless was all around — and I left myself and was gone.

I don't remember what it was like being gone. I remember being startled back by a voice from the house calling me in because it was my bedtime. It was like the raw agony of recovering from frostbite.

I believe it is exceptional to have had only one experience of this sort of thing during a whole childhood. But I was an unimaginative child — solitary and agnostic as a little cat, and mistrusting other children to a pitch of abhorrence, as cats do. Adults, if unfamiliar, often had charms. There was, for instance, Major Beldam — an unforgotten brief garden ornament.

Major Beldam was, as my mother's fashion magazine would have put it, a simple confection in red and grey. His face was red, he wore a suit of grey flannel — baggy and rather grubby. His pale-blue eyes were bloodshot. He was a large heavy man and walked with a limp. He had a grey walrus moustache. He owned a small unprofitable estate in Dumfriesshire, called Wolfshawes, and during the greater part of the year he lived there, supporting life on porridge and whisky, reading *The Field*, and singing 'Annie Laurie'. This I learned when I was older and have no warrant for the truth of it. All I knew at the time he came into the garden was that he made a yearly trip south to watch cricket matches at Lord's and, as we lived conveniently near London, invited himself to stay with us — which my mother resented and my father encouraged, laying in more whisky, addressing him, *Scotice*, as Wolfshawes, and trying to water down my mother's resentment by saying that Wolfshawes had no harm in him, and wasn't a classical scholar, and called a snapdragon a snapdragon, and hadn't got a wife

60

with legs like a horse, and was in every way more congenial than Scudamore, besides being merely occasional.

As Major Beldam was busy all day with cricket matches, and as I had to be in bed by half past six, I knew him mainly as a loud voice and a heavy tread and the concomitant phenomena of my mother raising her eyebrows and the maidservants giggling. But cricket matches were not played on Sundays, and early one Sunday morning there was a thump on my night-nursery door and a husky voice saying, 'I say, little girl — what's your name? Sylvie? — you shouldn't be in bed on a morning like this. Hurry up and dress yourself! Don't waste time on washing. It's a splendid morning — too good to miss.' I wasted no time on washing. Outside my door was Major Beldam with a finger to his walrus moustache. 'Come on out,' said he. 'Sh-h-h! Not a word.'

It did not seem a moment for the front door. I led him down the kitchen stairs and out by the back door, past the dustbins and so into the garden.

The garden had that brand-new look of early morning. The morning had the unmistakable reserve of a Sunday. I allowed Major Beldam his coup d'oeil. Then I began to show him round. Calculating my effects, I began with the dark path and the builder's yard; halting him among the horseradish I pointed out the exact spot by the hepaticas where my two dormice lay buried. As there was nothing to say about the rubbish heap, I said, 'This is the rubbish heap,' and showed off the flowerpots and detached a few snails for him to look at. The snails did not keep him long; when he had replaced them we turned sharply to the left, past the hop vine growing on the Wilbrahams' wall, past the Gloire de Dijon, and turned once again into the vista of the light path and the view beyond the dividing fence. Here I repeated to him a poem our cat had composed, in a rather 'Moab is my washpot' tone, about the Scudamores' garden. Then we came to the almond tree, and the lilies, and the kitchen window, where I picked him a sprig of sweetbriar to rub in his fingers.

61

It seemed to me that I had earned my reward. It was disconcerting when Major Beldam exclaimed, 'Now let's play at desert islands!'

Condescending to his childishness, I replied, 'Let's.'

'The first thing to do,' said he, 'is to build a fire to frighten away crocodiles.' Limping about the garden he collected twigs and stalks and tufts of dry grass and an old bird's nest, and supplemented these by raiding the dustbins and coming back with a quantity of straw bottle cases, potato peelings, newspaper, and a handkerchief full of cinders. With these additions he laid a fire in the middle of the central prairie. Bypassing that nonsense about crocodiles, I said, 'Let's cook something. Wait till I get a frying pan.' I came back with the frying pan and some dripping and a kipper which was lying about in the larder serving no useful purpose. Major Beldam charged the frying pan, settled it in, and lit the fire, which went out. He knelt down, relit the fire, and puffed. As he knelt down, he groaned, and between the puffs he continued to groan. Without a shade of compassion, but seeing my reward almost within my grasp, I said consolingly, 'Does it hurt, your poor leg?' He said it hurt like the devil but couldn't be helped. I didn't want philosophy, I wanted certainty. Tuning my rapacity to tones of dovelike concern, I asked if I might see it. He looked astonished but touched. Rising from his knees with more groans, he rolled up a grey flannel trouser leg over a hairy calf and displayed a varicose ulcer. I gazed. I made small moans of sympathy. And Major Beldam said I was a kind child, and rolled up more trouser leg to display the ulcer to better advantage.

Unwatched, the frying pan heeled over. The kipper and the dripping spilled into the fire, which blazed up. Wreaths of kipper-scented smoke rose into the morning air, crackles and splutterings broke the Sunday silence; and a window was thrown up with a bang and Mr. and Mrs. Scudamore leaned out and saw Major Beldam in the posture of a martyr, exhibiting his leg to my enraptured gaze. . . . A moment later, a matching window opened, and my parents

62

saw Major Beldam, etc. But as they also saw the Scudamores seeing it, they refrained from comment. And remarkably little was said about it afterwards.

How I Left the Navy

EARLY in my life my mother dedicated me to the British Navy—for the winter months, that is to say, and as far as possible. I was a little girl, and at that date little girls in England had not attained to trousers. From the waist down, therefore, I remained a member of the general public, wearing above my long, brown woollen legs a short knife-pleated skirt of blue serge. The British Navy began with a sturdy square-cut coat—a coat in which one might meet the battle and the breeze—made of solid dark-blue cloth, double-breasted, fastened with brass buttons, and called a reefer. On my head I wore a hat such as British sailors wear: a circular and flattened navy-blue bun supported on a stiff band about an inch wide. Round the band was a black silk ribbon with short, dangling ends, and emblazoned on the ribbon in gold letters was the name of one or another of His Majesty's ships of war: H.M.S. *Formidable*, or H.M.S. *Medusa*, or some such. The bun was kept on by a strip of black elastic passing under the chin and usually considerably too tight for comfort. Actually, this elastic was incorrect. Our bluejackets do not at any time wear elastic, either under their chins or under their back hair. Maybe it would be a help if they did when meeting the battle and the breeze.

Why my mother dedicated me to the British Navy, I cannot say. It might have been from patriotic motives, or because my second cousin by marriage once removed had been an admiral and one of the first members of the British Navy to bring back a chow dog from China on a battleship, or because when my mother was a girl she danced with naval officers and found them good dancers. Or the reasons for this dedication may have been more practical. I was the kind of child that does not respond to light colours and delicate tailoring, and I was also hard on my clothes. I had an experimental disposition and a strong inclination towards gutters, ditches, newly tarred gates, and excitable dogs with large paws. When I was costumed by the Admiralty, the wear and tear was not so noticeable.

Even so, of course, I grew out of my clothes, but I did not grow out of the British Navy. Winter after winter new reefer coats were bought for me and new navy-blue buns; the only thing that varied was the attribution on the ribbon that went round the bun.

I wish I could remember the names of the various ships of the line to which I rated. There was H.M.S. *Agamemnon*, I believe — at any rate the spelling seems strangely and deeply familiar — and some *Thunderbolts* and *Terribles* and *Tigers*. Nice names. I had no objection to them.

And then one day everything happened. I had come in from my afternoon walk, no dirtier than usual, and wearing my nautical clothes, and redolent of ocean breezes because I had carried back a little bag of shrimps for nursery tea (on the whole I had a very happy childhood), and my nurse had gone downstairs with the shrimps, and the clock in the hall was getting ready with groans and wheezes to strike four, and I was looking around for the cat in order to tell it about the shrimps. And suddenly my mother shot out of the drawing-room as though she had been shot from a gun. Her face was pale and her eyes were blazing and wrath had made her as uncommunicative as any high-explosive shell. There was a moment of impact in which it seemed to me that I was completely done for and during which the cat went upstairs like an arpeggio passage in a cadenza. I felt the navy-blue bun snatched from my head. The elastic twanged over my ears and past my chin. And when I re-opened my eyes I saw my mother rip the ribbon from the bun, cast them both on the floor, and stamp on them.

After she had stamped a while, she picked up the ruins

and went back to the drawing-room, remarking over her shoulder, 'You'll never wear that again!'

So much was clear. Whatever that cap was called, *Tiger* or *Galatea*, *Typhoon* or *Terrible*, it was past further wearing. But the rest of the incident was a mystery to me.

I put it away among the other mysteries. I asked no questions, and when on the morrow I was given a hat of beaver felt and found the reefer jacket considerably transformed by horn buttons in the place of brass buttons and a little strip of fur sewn on the collar, I made no comment. The beaver felt had elastic, too; the world held on its old course.

Ten years later my mother and I were in London doing some shopping, and we went past a store that I recognized.

'Isn't that where you used to buy my sailor caps?'

'Horrible, disgusting place! Loathsome firm!' said my mother with energy.

I thought of various possible reasons for my mother's frame of mind. Maybe she knew that the employees worked under bad conditions. Maybe she knew something against the character of the chairman of the board of directors. Maybe the store had a restaurant and she had been served with a discreditable curry there. Maybe there had been some altercation about matching buttons. It seemed best to say, quite simply, 'Why?'

'From the moment I set eyes on Mrs. Perivale,' said my mother, 'I knew she was a prize cat. She knew I knew it, too.'

'Was Mrs. Perivale that woman who lived in the house called Linden Lodge and gave religious garden parties, and you hated going to them? I didn't know she had anything to do with a store.'

'She didn't,' said my mother. 'She didn't have anything to do with me for long, either.'

'No?'

'All those pious women,' continued my mother, 'have filthy minds. I said to her that afternoon, after she had told me about that ship, "How fortunate that you should know so much about the seamy side of the Navy. I have always preferred to think of our battleships in mid-ocean, doing our business in the deep waters. I should not care to brood over the degradation of such a proud, clean thing as a battleship." That's what I said.'

'Which battleship?'

'The one on your cap, of course. Don't you remember how I took it away and never let you wear it again?'

'Yes, I remember. But I never quite knew why.'

'I couldn't tell you at the time,' said my mother. 'But you're old enough to be told about it now. Mrs. Perivale came to call that afternoon. And after simpering and rambling on and on and chewing her venomous cud, she said she felt she ought to tell me that the ship on your cap wasn't used as a battleship any longer. It was moored somewhere or other and used as a hospital ship for sailors with venereal disease. Just the sort of thing she would know!

'I've never been near that store since,' continued my mother. 'Disgusting place! What a trick to play on an innocent child!'

Madame Houdin

TWICE a week, on Tuesday and Friday afternoons, Madame Houdin came to our house in outer London to teach me French. Whether it was wet (when she would wear her brown dress) or fine (when she was apt to wear her tartan), Madame Houdin was always exactly punctual. First she would kiss me on either cheek. Then she would ask after my health. Then she would ask after my parents' health. Then I would ask after her health and after the health of Monsieur Houdin. Then she would say a few words to the dog. Then we would settle down, soberly, to enjoy ourselves.

Our enjoyment was always of a sober cast. We took life seriously, both of us. Except for addressing me as *chère petite*, Madame Houdin gave no acknowledgment to the gap of thirty years between our ages. I was ten. Not that she was incapable of unbending; when she talked to the dog it was always on light and simple subjects, but when she talked to me she addressed me as a rational being, with dignity, with earnestness, and with realism.

We discussed the problems of her life in a foreign land: the price of coffee, the risk entailed in taking unfamiliar purgatives, the frivolity of English butchers. Recommending a decoction of nut leaves for clearing the skin and finding that I had never heard of such things, Madame Houdin would shake her head and say that the English had no feeling for nature. We discussed, too, the difficulties of being married to a husband twenty years one's senior. 'Naturally,' said Madame Houdin, 'he now begins to realize that he will leave me a widow. He saddens himself over this.

And to be consoling on such a subject requires a certain tact.'

I learned by degrees that in his anxiety to leave a widow well provided for, Monsieur Houdin was inclined to stint a wife, and together we would analyse the condition of Madame Houdin's boots and debate as to how she could most painlessly extract the price of a new pair. It was a serious sum, for to be reliable and solid, boots must be expensive, and since not only one's health but one's emotions, too, are conditioned by one's footwear, boots must be both reliable and solid.

Cheap boots were no more intolerable than cheap black, however, and from Madame Houdin I acquired a discriminating respect for *un beau noir*. That was why Madame Houdin wore brown on wet days, tartan on fine days. *Un beau noir* and its upkeep were too expensive for everyday wearing. 'Cats,' said she, 'who dress themselves at the establishment of Nature, can afford to wear black in all weathers, all circumstances. But even they must titivate continually.'

But prudence and parsimony alike were brushed away by the wing of death. One Tuesday after the summer holidays, Madame Houdin appeared in a black so black, in a veil so ample, that for a moment I felt sure Monsieur Houdin must be dead. It was, however, Monsieur Houdin's brother who had died. With gusto, with exactitude, with Miltonic fluency, Madame Houdin described the course of his mortal sickness and swept on to the funeral: the perfection of the weather, the number of the attenders, the beauty of the mourning tributes.

'We offered a wreath, a superb wreath made entirely of beads. That endures!'

Funeral wreaths of beads were something I had never heard of before, and I asked to hear more. At learning the price, remembering Monsieur Houdin's anxiety to leave a well-dowered widow. I must have looked my astonishment.

'We were content,' she said, 'to pay so much. One does not grudge to the dead.'

She herself did not grudge to the living, either. What she lacked in means she made up for in ingenuity. Coffee and biscuits accompanied the French lessons, and she always gathered up the biscuit crumbs and put them in an envelope, carried in her bag, so that she might feed the sparrows who came to her window box.

The contents of Madame Houdin's bag were a great pleasure to us both. It was a large, sack-shaped bag made of dark-purple velvet — the remnant of an earlier splendour — and tied with a drawstring. Inside were several spare handkerchiefs, a box of cough lozenges, a bottle of smelling salts, pencils and pencil sharpeners, a needlecase and scissors, a pin box, a pair of spare bootlaces, two different pairs of eyeglasses, a rather neglected rosary, various safety pins, a small bottle of eau de cologne, a tape measure, a photograph of Monsieur Houdin, remedies against colds and against indigestion, a roll of sticking plaster, Madame Houdin's thimble and another thimble which had belonged to Madame Houdin's mother, nickel medals of St. Anthony and St. Christopher and St. Joseph, a bottle of iodine, several neat little rolls of string, the envelope with crumbs for the birds, a small enamel box containing caraway seeds, a spare pair of gloves, three different purses, an assortment of season tickets, a buttonhook, a brandy flask, a collection of coloured picture postcards of the most renowned buildings of France, a stout tag inscribed with Madame Houdin's name and address and the number of her life-insurance policy, a powder compact, and a comb.

These were the permanent fittings of Madame Houdin's bag. Among its more fleeting contents were bananas, birdseed, lumps of sugar for tired cart horses, darning wool and a sock or two of Monsieur Houdin's, and chop bones wrapped in wax paper, in case Madame Houdin met a deserving and needy dog.

In the midst of all these was Madame Houdin's copy, in one stout volume, of *Les Trois Années de la Grammaire*. And sooner or later she would pull it out, with the remark that one must also work a little.

The *Three Years of Grammar* was a textbook used in French public schools. Rules, glosses, exercises, therefore, were all in French, obediently to Madame Houdin's contention that there must be no miscegenation, no crossbreeding of tongues. The result of this theory, in my case at least, was a singularly patchy control of the French language. Some things became clear to me, others remained a mystery. To this day, if I were roused from my sleep by an inquiry as to the plural form of the French for 'jackal'. I could supply it instantly and correctly. I am also, I think, pretty sound on the distinction between *les Pâques* (*chrétiens*) and *la pâque* (*judaïque*), and every now and then I astonish myself and others by the classical elegance of my subjunctives. I gathered, in fact, a sort of hothouse collection from the grammar of France. I am tolerable among the orchids but lost in the kitchen garden.

Two other factors, besides the factor of studying unknown rules in a partially unknown tongue, unsettled my hold on French grammar. One was that Madame Houdin decided in a lighthearted manner that as the *First Year of Grammar* was designed for infants, I, being past the age of infancy, need not study it. I began, therefore, not with the rules but with the exceptions — among the jackals and the *bains-marie* and the surviving forms of the extinct verb '*gésir*.' The other factor was even more dishevelling — and equally the result of a certain wilfulness in Madame Houdin's temperament. Her copy of the *Three Years of Grammar* was of an earlier vintage than mine. It was, in fact, *hors la loi*, as it embodied a great deal of religious and social opinion which, on later developments in the Republic, the Ministry of Education had expunged from the public curriculum, substituting other subjects and other points of view.

Accordingly, while I was doing my best to distinguish between the occasions proper for the *passé défini* and those proper for the *passé indéfini*, everything would be darkened by the fact that while Madame Houdin's edition

71

recounted the building of the Chapelle Expiatoire, mine had a powerful description of the downfall of the absinthe drinker. Where Madame Houdin's edition spoke of the merits of the saints, mine expatiated on the value of chemical manures, and while I was reading that the weevil is a scourge of the agriculturist, she would come clashing in with the statement that freemasons undermine the base of society.

This was not only confusing, it was interesting. Much more interesting, both to Madame Houdin and myself, than mere grammar. Presently the warring textbooks were put by and Madame Houdin would launch full-sailed into the *Affaire Dreyfus*, or the expulsion of the Jesuits, or the Panama scandal, or the Camelots du Roi. By means of the *Three Years of Grammar* I learned thirty years of French history—sketchily enough and sketched with considerable prejudice, but sketched with the look of life. I learned, too, how, beneath Madame Houdin's patient hold on everyday things, the price of coffee and of boots, the grace of tact one must pay to a faithful but difficult husband, the validity of biscuit crumbs and chop bones in the scheme of society, the blackness of black, and the enduring value-for-money of beads, there ran this impassioned concern for the destiny of France. It was as though a living body had been opened and I were shown how the thrifty, busy hand, the trudging feet, the black eyes, and nimble tongue are fed and animated by the violent machine of the heart.

Siegfried on the Rhine

MY grandmother, knowing her own mind as usual, had gone to Cortina d'Ampezzo as fast as trains could carry her, to await us in civilized surroundings, she said, while we dawdled our way through Germany. My mother had never seen Germany, whereas she had frequently seen her mother-in-law, and to please my mother we began our dawdle through Germany with a journey up the Rhine. That is how we came to be sitting in the public gardens of Coblenz on a Sunday in July in the year 1908.

The town band was playing. All around the bandstand were ranks of little metal tables each with three or four metal chairs, and though the band was playing with great volume and amplitude, and though the listeners were engaged in loud and happy conversations, the noise of band and listeners combined was quite often swamped by the noise of the metal chairs grating on the gravel as the family parties at the little tables got up to greet their friends or to call on waiters. Over our heads was a reef of plane tree boughs, quite notably silent, for there was not a breath of air.

And so we sat at our little table while the band played its way through a succession of massive potpourris, and my mother fanned herself in time with the band, since there was nothing else for her idle hands to do. Most of the ladies of Coblenz had brought their Sunday needlework with them. My father and I were feeling less conspicuous, as we were drinking beer; a matter of deep satisfaction to us both, for it signified a victory over my mother's determination to boil all the child's drinking water in case of typhoid. It was my third day as an infant alcoholic. I was quite accustomed to my state, and had even left off feeling belittled at the sight of children demonstrably younger than myself also drinking beer. My mother fanned herself, my father sat draped around his metal chair looking like a black puma in an hour of ease, the potpourri oscillated ponderously between dominant and tonic and came to a close.

There was a pause. The players spruced themselves, the horns emptied their instruments with particular attention, the drummer interrogated his drums. The conductor rose with a stern expression, gathered his instrumentalists, loosened his shoulders, and launched into the Funeral March from *The Twilight of the Gods.*

With a roar of gravel as when an Atlantic wave hits the beach, metal chairs were thrust back and all the men present rose to their feet and stood bareheaded at attention. So did my father. So would my mother and I have done, but he waved us down, to sit in conformity with the indigenous women and children.

For the puma was an ardent Wagnerian. Sachs could not muse too thoroughly for him, nor Wotan appear too often or stay too long. He loved Wagner as much as he disliked Germans. It was a matter of personal resentment to him that a nation that otherwise afforded Europe no manifestations of being much troubled by having music in its soul should have been allowed by some miscarrying providence to produce *Tristan* and *The Ring.* But now, while the players clashed and swam through the résumé of Siegfried's heroic career, he began to eat his words and make an amend. These exasperating Germans must be better than they seemed. Somewhere under that bellicose and pettifogging exterior there lay a genuine sensibility. For here they were, rising unprompted from their Sunday repose to honour a noble piece of music.

The Funeral March came to an end, the males of Coblenz sat down again, the band had a drink and set off

74

on a polka, the waiters brought more mugs and more mats, the ladies embroidered on. But my father looked at all this with new eyes. After all, and little as the rest of the afternoon bore it out, there was music in their souls. Presently he began to talk to a gentleman at a neighbouring table, saying that it was a fine performance of the Funeral March.

'Yes, indeed,' said the gentleman warmly. 'Very fine. It was played as a tribute to our town clerk, who died last week, the unfortunate man! But how strange that you should know this music. The English are not a musical people.'

Pumas, after a momentary loss of balance, go walking along the bough with increased blandness, more impenetrable suavity. Just as did my father, talking with his new acquaintance, display a courteous interest in the life and death of an exemplary functionary.

A Golden Legend

I READ not long ago in a pious weekly that the sentence 'In my Father's house are many mansions' has been causing disquiet and confusion to modern readers, a state of things that a new translation of the Gospels will redress by substituting for the word 'mansions' some religious synonym for flats. I can foresee trouble on this score, too — a dangerous Westernization of an Eastern image — but I will not go into it now; all I wish to say is that the sentence has never caused me any trouble, because my Great-Uncle Augustine's house was after the same pattern, and in my youth I often heard about it.

Great-Uncle Augustine married my grandfather's sister. I have a photograph of him — a *carte de visite*, taken about the date of the marriage. He is quite astonishingly handsome, tall and slender, with classical features and classical whiskers — the kind of whisker that frames the jaw but does not intrude on mouth or chin — and his attitude, as he leans, in his long sleek clerical coat and well-cut clerical waistcoat, on the back of a chair looking down on the open book in his hand, emphasizes his graceful build and port. Pensive, elegant, high-minded, he looks like a stanza in 'In Memoriam'; and it would seem well-nigh inevitable (though in fact nothing of the sort occurred) that the Church of England would lead him onwards into becoming not a bishop — a tougher fibre is required for bishops — but that better, lovelier thing, a dean. There is a companion photograph of Great-Aunt Rosie, and she, too, is tall and slender. But the poet she calls to mind is not Tennyson. She looks like Lamia in a crinoline. They loved, they married on very adequate means, they had a succession of beautiful high-spirited children — in all, I believe, sixteen.

By the time the total had reached double figures, the house was becoming inconveniently animated, so Augustine threw out two wings, or pavilions, or what term you will; but, in essence, mansions. In the right-hand mansion he disposed his older sons with a tutor; in the left-hand mansion, his older daughters with a governess; and in the main fabric he and his wife enjoyed a quiet domesticity, with a considerable staff of servants, a housekeeper called Pincher, and just three or four little ones.

The whole family, of course, was often gathered together — for household prayers, for birthdays and feasts of the church, for Sunday supper. It was at a Sunday supper that Augustine, while carving a cold turkey, held up a sinewy drumstick on a fork and said, 'Now, boys, what does this remind you of?' Before they could reply, he answered the question himself, in the tones of one assured, 'Pincher's leg.' This took place in the home circle; no one was the worse for it. Sometimes, however, Augustine's wide-ranging mind would take a flight during the rectory dinner parties, and when it ranged too far, his Rosie had to collect the attention of the female guests, rise, and shepherd them away into the drawing-room. There, she went round from lady to lady, saying confidentially, 'You must forgive dear Augustine. You see, he is so steeped in the classics.'

But I do not think so meanly of the Church of England as to suppose that it withheld the apron for this. Augustine was subject to cataplexy — a malady summarized by the medical dictionary as 'a sudden temporary loss of muscular tone in which the patient collapses,' and which compels him to lie speechless and seemingly unconscious till the attack passes and allows him to get up and go about his business as usual. The family had learned to take these fits in their stride, and servants were trained to do likewise, so

77

that a footman bringing the teakettle, or a note on a salver, knew that he must step over the prostrate form with a respectful absence of comment; for though the cataplectic may appear to be unconscious, their imprisoned faculties are sharp as ever, and Augustine was rather touchy about his fits. But no doubt the ecclesiastical authorities thought that it would be more difficult to train a whole band of cathedral clergy and functionaries to step over their dean, especially if a ceremony was going on and the clergy were impeded by their skirts. Ladies could lift up a skirt and show an ankle, and look the more charming for it. Canons in residence, no. Not at that date, anyhow.

By the date I was hearing about these interesting relations, quite a number of people were inclined to think that such a heredity should not have been distributed among quite so many children. They were wrong. Only one of the children died untimely, and he of scarlet fever. Only one of them inherited the malady, and she, as far as I know, only once gave an exhibition of it. Still, the circumstances were unfortunate. A young man, the son of a widow, had asked her to marry him, she had agreed to do so, and the young man's mother had asked her to tea. The affair had taken place with such rapidity that this was Thekla's first meeting with her prospective mother-in-law. Feeling decidedly nervous, she entered the room and saw a sweet-faced woman coming hospitably towards her. The widow was short. Thekla was tall. She looked down into a pair of spectacles. 'And you are Thekla! I am so—' The widow said no more. Thekla could not say anything. She was lying on the floor, with something beneath her that struggled and moaned. Powerless to move, unable to utter a syllable of regret, she watched sons and servants rush into the room, heard cries of 'Send for the doctor!' By the time the doctor came, she was beyond his help, for she had recovered. But he did not come in vain, for Thekla had broken her hostess's leg.

'It is so particularly unfortunate that this should have happened to Thekla, who is gentler than the other dear

78

girls, and feels quite crushed by it all.' So wrote Rosie in a letter to my grandmother, whose comment was, 'Slipshod thinking'. And indeed, though the dear girls were beautiful, graceful, talented, warmhearted, dressed in the height of fashion, and fervently religious, they were none of them gentle. A friend of the family said that when they came into the room, all lovely and all talking at once, it was like being descended on by a flight of angels. Angels in flight are not gentle. They sweep on their way, each angel single-mindedly bent on what it means to do next. In the case of Veronica, who, being a couple of inches shorter than her sisters, was known as Tiddlywinks, piety took an evangelical turn. She used to go slumming among the London poor — accompanied, of course, by a lady's maid — and, stationing herself at a street corner or outside a public house, she would play the fiddle till a crowd gathered. Then she would hand the fiddle to the lady's maid and preach. The converts were many, and often a train of them would follow her till she reached a cab rank and got into a four-wheeler. For at that date no young lady — not even when accompanied by a lady's maid, not even when followed by a train of converts — could reputably drive off in a hansom.

The sisters had swarms of admirers, collectively and individually, and eventually they all got married, though they were so happy and interested at home that they were in no hurry to do so. In the meantime, they were in constant demand as bridesmaids. Augustine, looking so noble in his surplice, was in as constant demand as chief clergyman — the Church of England allows the solemnization of matrimony to be apportioned among several clergymen, one doing one thing, another another, so if he had happened to be struck down among the lilies, there would always have been a cockhorse clergyman to replace him — and weddings, apart from those of parishioners, were constantly taking place in his church, for the aisle was wide, and Rosie threw herself heart and soul into wedding breakfasts. For one of these weddings, the bridesmaids' hats were sent from Paris. Like everything sent from Paris, they arrived after their arrival had been despaired of, superlatively packed in reams of tissue paper and on the very eve of the ceremony. Six hats were lifted from six bandboxes, and immediately a schism arose. Which way round were they to be worn? Were the white roses clustered under the green brims to be in front or at the back, over the nose or over the knot? Cecilia, Veronica, Agatha, Sabina, Rufina, and Frideswide sat up till sunrise vehemently debating this question. Each knew her own mind, each was ready to die for her faith. Each came down to breakfast hollow-eyed but unyielding, the debate continued, everyone in the house became drawn into it, and by the time it occurred to Pincher that a telegram of inquiry could be sent to the bride, it was too late to send it. Moberley, one of the brothers, suggested tossing up. This united the controversialists, who said it was too utterly cynical. When the bride approached the church, she saw, lined up in the porch to receive her, three clusters of white roses over three aquiline noses, three over Grecian knots. A second glance showed her that it would not do to assert herself, and, tightening her hold on her father's arm, she went with dignity up the aisle.

It will be observed by anyone with a scrap of hagiology about him that the daughters of this house had names drawn from the Calendar of the Saints. Augustine chose them. In the case of Merivale, Moberley, Ridley, Faber, Grote, Stone, and Fazackerley (Augustine gracefully left the boys for Rosie to name) the system is less apparent, the chime more recondite; but a clue runs through them, whereas it is difficult to see how anyone should leap from Rufina to Frideswide, unless by means of a pin. Rosie's choice of Merivale, Moberley, etc., had hagiological implications, too. It commemorated a series of young men who had successively inserted themselves into the canon of what she called her 'Special Dears.' In a sense they were Augustine's Dears, too, since they were his pupils, and a considerable source of his income. Even before his marriage he was doing well as a coach, and as a married coach he did even better, taking not only young men who wanted to study theology or be steeped in the classics but those whose parents thought their health needed special attention or their character a more sheltered climate than they would find at a university. Such parents, led into the drawing-room to be introduced to Rosie, finding her with Baby Thekla in her lap, Cecilia and Veronica at foot, seeing the look of heartbreak that crossed her face when they spoke of Algie's kidneys, hearing her compassionating 'How sad!' when they mentioned Frank's inability to keep proper accounts, admired their own acumen in finding such an ideal establishment, and in reply to her assurances that she would watch over their dear boys like a mother told her they knew she would.

And so she did, taking a deep interest in their lungs, their underwear, their souls, their aspirations, their news from home, and writing very long letters at least once a week to report on their health, analyse their dispositions, dilate on their progress or, if that was not possible, dwell on hopeful signs, all in a rapid sloping hand and with a command of language that did her great credit — the more so since she was in the habit of dashing off these letters at the breakfast table, at the same time dealing with a reiteration of coffee cups, sending messages to the cook, and appeasing Augustine's morning pettishness. Her heart went out to all of them, she said, and Algie's kidneys and Frank's bill at the tailor's had a like place in her prayers. But naturally she found some one among them more interesting than the others, more interesting and more responsive, better fitted to read aloud 'The Blessed Damozel' and listen to Chopin in the April twilight, more in need of her sympathy, perhaps, or possibly more grateful. They came, they went, and whenever the opportunity of a male infant allowed it she commemorated them. Merivale, Moberley, Ridley, Faber, Grote, Stone, and Fazackerley. When the tenure of the current Special Dear coincided with the birth of a daughter, nothing could be done. Her last-born son she named Augustine, but the tribute was soon obliterated under the pet name of Bunnikin. Coming belatedly at the tail of such a long family, Bunnikin was almost my contemporary. I remember a day—I was staying at my grandparents'—when Bunnikin was to be brought over to play with me, conveyed by some of his sisters. They were making a party of it; one of the many admirers was driving them over in his brake. I remember the arrival, the angels descending from the brake, their hats, their profiles, their fragrance, the rustle of their petticoats, their voices mingling in a melodious full cry, falsely mournful like a cry of hounds. 'And here's Bunnikin. Bunnikin, Bunnikin! But where's Bunnikin? Where *is* our sweet little Bunnikin?' Bunnikin had been left behind.

I wish I had seen more of this family. My mother could not tolerate them; she said they made her head whirl, that they were a religious circus, a nest of fireworks, Bedlam Unbound, Pandemonium let loose; she also said that Rosie was an archliar and archhypocrite, and that no man was safe within a mile of her. Honour would then compel her to admit that few women could have endured such a gruelling life and come out of it with head so unbowed, spirits so unabated, and such a figure. Perhaps if the head had been more bowed, the spirits and the waistline lost, my mother would have felt more tolerance. Great-Aunt Rosie was an old woman, long widowed, living alone, and writing her innumerable letters on paper increasingly black-edged as first her contemporaries died and then her juniors, when, after an interval of many years, she reappeared among us, announcing herself on the telephone as being in the neighbourhood, and saying she would like to come to tea on the morrow. 'Thank God your father will be out!' my mother exclaimed. However, he changed his plans, and was in. When the old Lamia, who had actually worn a crinoline, rose up to depart, she dropped a glove. I bent to pick it up. But, sweeping down like a willow wand from a height that well overtopped mine, she reached it before me.

Though, even in my youth, she was more legend than woman to me, and now is almost wholly legend, I am still liable to become vividly aware of her — as though she were leaning over my shoulder while I say down the telephone, 'Wednesday? I would have adored to, but I've got to be out all day,' or 'I was so sorry not to be there, but I had the most appalling cold in my head — and I still haven't got rid of it,' or 'But if you can't send the chops in time for lunch, we shall have absolutely nothing to eat.' For the family voice, that mysterious arrangement of molecules, is speaking. And it gives me a touching sense of security to hear it again, and to know that while I cannot claim to be an archliar and archhypocrite, I am yet in the tradition.

A Correspondence in
The Times

MY Aunt Angel was paying one of her visits to London, a winter visit in her skunk. As usual, she had a little shopping to do, and my mother and I went shopping with her.

On this afternoon we had been to Marshall & Snelgrove, Penberthy (for gloves), D. H. Evans, Waring & Gillow, Peter Robinson, Liberty's (for a wedding present), The Goldsmiths' Company (repair to Aunt Angel's teapot), and Robinson & Cleaver. We had also visited a very small shop in an alley off Great Marlborough Street, where Aunt Angel always buys buttons, and an exhibition of garden water colours, and we had looked in at Burlington House. Now we were having tea at Stewart's, at a small table so beset with boxes, parcels, and small chintz-paper bags that the waitress who brought the toast and the tea had the greatest difficulty in placing them on the table. Indeed, there was a moment when it seemed that the neat gentleman at the next table, who for his part had no entanglements save with an umbrella, was likely to get Aunt Angel's toast before she did.

'After tea,' said Aunt Angel, 'I want to see those California floods at the cinema.'

'I only hope,' said my mother, 'that we shan't be seeing our own. I don't know what's come over the Thames. It seems to be much further up the Embankment than it used to be.'

'It's the moon. Don't you remember Flora's face in India?'

The family voice is loud, the family diction is clear. The gentleman at the next table looked up with interest. I was interested too, and asked, 'What happened to Flora's face?'

'She went to sleep in the moonlight,' Aunt Angel explained. 'I suppose the ayah had not closed the shutters properly. Anyhow, it was a full moon and she slept in it, and when she woke, one side of her face was so swelled that she couldn't open that eye.'

'Which Flora was that?' inquired my mother, pretty calmly.

'Flora McCuddy. In Madras.'

'It can't have been Flora McCuddy. Flora McCuddy never was in Madras. It must have been Flora Popham. Or else it was at Jubbulpore, not Madras.'

'Nonsense, Nora. It was Flora McCuddy, because I can distinctly remember her telling me about the mad dog that nearly bit Captain Kimmins. And that was at Madras.'

'Flora Popham,' repeated my mother. 'I suppose you know that Tottie Larpent is dead?'

Two days later Aunt Angel exclaimed, 'Have you seen this extraordinary coincidence in *The Times*?'

The letter was headed 'Lunar Gravity,' and ran as follows:

SIR:

The recent level of the Thames at Westminster Bridge suggests to me that your readers might be interested in another example of the power which can be exercised by the moon at its full. A lady of my acquaintance, now unfortunately no more, told me that when she was in Madras she inadvertently slept with the light of the brilliant full moon of Southern India upon one side of her face. In the morning the cheek on which the moonlight had rested was distended and highly painful, and so perceptible was the influence of lunar gravity that for some time she was unable to open one eye. I should be interested to know if any of your readers have had similar experiences.

JUNIOR CARLTON CLUB   AUTOLYCUS

'Just what I told you, Nora. Flora McCuddy.'

'Flora Popham,' said my mother.

They argued with some briskness. Flora McCuddy and

Flora Popham and Captain Kimmins and the mad dog and several other figures from the family past were whirled round in the debate, and Aunt Angel regretted that a photograph album which would, she said, have settled everything was in Devonshire, so carefully put away that it was not possible to indicate its whereabouts by a telegram. On the morrow they rustled through *The Times* but found nothing more to the point than a letter from some crank or other about sowing turnips in the wax of the moon. The next day brought a much better bag. Besides two letters on turnips and a letter from a lady in Cheltenham saying that an Indian full moon was something which those who had only viewed the moon from Europe could not imagine, Ethelberta Woolley-Wallis added her important testimony:

SIR,

On my first visit to Madras, now many years ago, I was warned by my ayah never to sleep in the light of a full moon. The result of doing this was not made quite clear, and I understood that a severe headache would be my portion if I were unwary enough to do so. But in the light of Autolycus's letter I now feel convinced that a swelling of the face might have resulted, and this, in those bygone days, would have been a serious matter to a young bride. My ayah was a most devoted and intelligent creature. I wonder, a little sadly, if a present-day ayah would be so devoted to the welfare of her mem-sahib, for there has been a most regrettable change for the worse in the relations of the white and coloured races, due (in my humble opinion) entirely to ill-advised kow-towing to misguided, if not worse, sedition-mongers.

'There, you see! Madras,' exclaimed Aunt Angel.

Meanwhile my mother's eye had gone further down the column, and she uttered a cry of triumph.

SIR:

I can add my corroboration to the story told by your correspondent, 'Autolycus'. 'I personally had a somewhat similar experience of the Indian full moon when I was in the Central Provinces in 1898. In my case I was 'sleeping rough' while on shikar, and as I closed my eyes and composed myself to slumber, hearing all round me the howlings and barkings of the jungle excited by the full moon, I remarked to my companion that I wondered if we should not find ourselves mauled before daylight. His reply was on some-what fatalistic lines, and we were speedily asleep. The light of our fire and the noise made by our beaters kept the animal life at a respectful distance. But on awaking I found myself in possession of the worst stiff neck it has ever been my lot to experience in the course of a pretty arduous and adventurous life, and my companion told me it was caused by the moon. Repressing a natural impulse to reply 'Moonshine,' I made further enquiries which fully bore out his diagnosis. No doubt only the difference between my tough skin and a lady's more delicate epidermis stood between me and such a swelling as described by 'Autolycus.'

CHOLMONDELEY COFFIN,

UNITED SERVICES CLUB   *Lieut. Col. retd.*

'Central Provinces! Jubbulpore! Of course it was Flora Popham,' said my mother. Aunt Angel seemed uncon-vinced by this reasoning, even when my mother added that everyone admitted that the heat in India grew hotter and hotter as one went inland and that therefore the inland moon must be stronger too. When Aunt Angel left by the 2:15 for Exeter, one would have thought that the two sisters, championing their respective Floras, would never again transcend terms of armed neutrality. Yet at that very moment, perhaps, the words had been penned which would unite them in a single thought, a single reaction. For the next day's *Times* carried (in addition to a trifl-ing communication from the gentleman who had read the Thirty-nine Articles in Cornwall by the light of the aurora borealis) a letter suggesting that a mosquito and not the moon might have been responsible for the swelled cheek of the lady in Madras. And in addition to this outrage, the third editorial, headed 'O, Swear Not by the Moon,' poked fun at the whole story in a demure, satirical way and insinuated that there might be a good deal to be said for the hypothesis of the mosquito.

87

The family honour was at stake. My mother and my Aunt Angel sprang to its defence. There was no leisure for consultation, no leisure for reconciliation even. But in Monday's *Times* they met.

SIR:

Your correspondent, J. Wilkins Metcalf, doubts the accuracy of the incident related by Autolycus. I am in a position to substantiate it, since the lady in question, Mrs. Wolf McCuddy, was my first cousin once removed. I can well recollect Mrs. McCuddy telling me of this experience and describing it as one of the most remarkable things that happened to her in Madras.

17 ROUGEMONT ROAD, EXETER   ANGEL BURBECK

SIR:

As regards the letter by Autolycus and the subsequent suggestion by Mr. Wilkins Metcalf that a mosquito and not the full moon was responsible, I happen to be able to settle the matter. The lady was my aunt by marriage, Mrs. Algernon Popham, and I have often heard the story from her lips, exactly as told by Autolycus except for one detail. Mrs. Popham was never in Madras. India is a continent, a fact often overlooked by those who have never been there, and contains many things quite as strange as this story which Mr. Wilkins Metcalf finds improbable. My aunt by marriage, who knew India well, would have been much amused at this suggestion that she had mistaken a moon-stroke for a mosquito bite.

32 SHEEPCOT TERRACE, W.8   NORA WARNER

'I think your letter is the more convincing,' I said to my mother. 'Aunt Angel has overdone the formality. Yours seems to me to ring truer.'

'I should hope so,' replied my mother. 'Poor Flora McCuddy! Why should Flora Popham's lies be fathered on her like that?'

'Flora Popham's lies?' said I.

'Just because she's been in India! As if no one else in the family had ever been in India. Full moon, indeed! If the full moon could bulge a brazen kettle, then I might believe that it bulged Flora Popham's cheek.'

'But, Mother, you said right along it was Flora Popham! Did she tell you this story?'

'Of course not,' said my mother. 'It's just one of Angel's woolgatherings. But I couldn't have such a silly story fastened on poor, honest, simple-hearted old Flora McCuddy.'

The Young Sailor

READING last week in some family papers how 'the Bishop did them in whole railsful with both hands' —my grandmother's fastidious Scotch account of a mass confirmation in St. Paul's—I was glad that the mellowing influence of some fifty years had intervened between the ceremony she described and a similar ceremony in which I played my modest part. If she had objected, her objection would have had the force of an ex cathedra; my grandfather had been well esteemed as a preacher and my grandmother had written all his sermons, which made her the family authority on matters of church discipline. But she did not object. I was confirmed in St. Paul's, and I do not in any way regret it.

I was sixteen at the time, and not in a state of religious exaltation. We were not a religious household. But the due preliminaries had been attended to. I had some conversations on theology with a clerical friend of my parents, a man of signal goodness of heart but without much dialectical address. (I remember him saying, 'And, of course, there's the Atonement.') My father ascertained that I was acquainted with the Thirty-Nine Articles and knew the Church Catechism by heart, and drew my attention to a text (Isaiah 40:31) that implies that it is less taxing and remarkable to mount up like eagles than to go on walking, which, considering the perseverance I had put into learning the Catechism, I thought unkind. My mother gave much anxious consideration to how I could possibly combine wearing a veil with wearing spectacles.

And on a fine May morning (I know it was in May; May is
90

an unlucky month for marriages but not for confirmations)
I was punctually in my place in the nave of St. Paul's
without an uneasy thought in my mind, for the incompati-
bility of my veil and my spectacles (I had insisted on
retaining the spectacles) was—as, thanks to the spectacles, I
soon discovered—a handicap shared by a number of other
candidates, and anything like stagefright was abolished by
my being one of such a number that all I had to do was to
do as all the others did. It was not as if I were in one of the
front rows. I was well situated, somewhere about the
middle. Best of all, there was no one within sight whom I
had ever set eyes on before.

I sat in tranquil anonymity, waiting for the Bishop to
appear and the service to begin. I listened to the organ,
which was rolling about in one of those somnolent extem-
porizations that Church of England organists do so well. I
looked towards the dome, and there it was. I glanced across
the central aisle, which sexually differentiated the candidates, and thought it was hard for boys not to be granted
veils; one feels so ensconced in a veil. Our parents,
godparents, and other confirmed members of the Church of
England sat well to the back of the building in, as it were, a
sort of hallowed pit, and this added to my satisfaction,
partly because it meant that my mother could not get at me
for any last-minute pinnings or admonitions, and partly
because it was agreeable to think of them being kept in their
place—a comfortable, respectable place, but not the opera-
tive one. My memory assures me that they were held back by
some red ropes. But I do not think this was actually the
case; the ropes were probably incorporeal. Anyhow, they
could not get in among us; they were no part of the flock.

I had very powerfully the sensation of being one of a
flock, in an exceedingly handsome fold. We were such a
large flock (I daresay there were five hundred of us, culled
from the metropolitan diocese, and perhaps more) that the
handsomeness of the fold did not seem beyond our deserts,
and yet, on the other hand, the fold's classical stature and
magnificence, and the absence of fuss with which Sir

Christopher Wren did his business, countervailed any tendency to self-importance or egoistic exaltation. It is in school chapels that confirmation candidates have visions and see doves hovering with marked solicitude over particular heads—usually their own heads. With the best will in the world (not that I was set on it, or thought it very likely), I could not anticipate such a distinguishing dove's being requisitioned for the ceremony about to take place. Flocking, I felt, was the main thing. And any specifically pious thoughts I had were all of security, continuity, and conformity, with a musing awareness that in the Book of Common Prayer the service of Confirmation is followed by the Solemnization of Matrimony, and that, in turn, by the Visitation of the Sick and the Burial of the Dead.

Meanwhile, the organ had rolled into a more purposeful measure, the Bishop had entered, and the service had begun.

In the Book of Common Prayer, the Order of Confirmation is brief and compact (making prudent allowance, as I had learned, for the length of time required for a Bishop's reiterated 'Defend, O Lord, this Thy Child,' etc.). I had been somewhat taken aback to discover from the leaflet provided that the Prayer Book text was to be considerably bulked out by the inclusion of hymns and two Addresses from the Bishop, one before the 'Defend, O Lord's, and one after—by which time, considering what railfuls there were of us, he might reasonably have been expected to be rather out of breath and disinclined for further talking. But it was not this that prejudiced me against the Bishop. It was his habiliments that I was disappointed in. Reared on the engravings of Gillray and Rowlandson, I had expected his lawn sleeves to be much puffier. I may even subconsciously have been expecting him to wear a full-bottomed wig. As it was, I judged that he looked meagre, and that his cassock should not have shown so much of his boots, and that those boots should not have been—however nicely blacked—such plainly secular boots. But the state of being in a flock, secured by those ropes and impersonally brooded over by

92

that ravishing echo, which turns the squeak of a chair into psalmody and into which coughs and sneezes ascend and are instantly beatified into mild hallelujahs, kept me in a decent frame of mind, and when the Bishop began his first Address, I took pains to sort him out from the squeaks, coughs, and sneezes, and to attend to what he might have to say.

'The Wages of Sin Is Death.' That was his text, and perhaps he thought we were not familiar with it, for he repeated it pretty frequently. I was thinking about the grammatical oddity, which at some time or other had been explained to me, and trying to recall the explanation, when a new ingredient was cast into the echo. It came from the further side of the sexually dividing aisle, and was contributed by a young man wearing the uniform of a rating in the Royal Navy. He was edging his way past the knees and among the feet and the hassocks of the half-dozen or so candidates seated between him and the aisle. Though he was doing it carefully and considerately, he could not do it silently, and his face wore that expression of contained, unwilling woe that designates the truebred Englishman when he knows he is making himself conspicuous. Once disentangled, however, he looked cheerful, and walked lightly and briskly down the aisle and eventually out of the building.

We were all too well-conducted to seem to notice this, and the Bishop was also too well-conducted to waver in his peroration or interpolate a pastoral recall. We behaved as though nothing had happened. But the recording echo had not failed to gather up those departing steps, and we were all of us perfectly aware that the young sailor had got up and gone away.

Afterwards my parents and I often discussed this strange incident, each of us, as usual, with his own theory. According to my mother, the young sailor had never meant to be confirmed. He had gone into St. Paul's for a little sightseeing and, finding it too much for him, had sat down in what was at that moment a nice, empty public building

and fallen asleep. A young sailor could sleep through anything; we had Shakespeare's word for it, and Shakespeare
was always right. So the young sailor slept on, peacefully as
though upon the high and giddy mast, while the confirmation candidates mustered round him, and the service began,
and got as far as halfway through the Bishop. Then,
catching some view-halloo note in the Bishop's oratory, the
young sailor had woken, realized his peril, and got out just
in time. Nelson would have been delighted — my mother
rated Nelson only one below Shakespeare. My father disagreed; in fact, he disagreed twice. My mother, he said,
took Shakespeare too literally, and did not make allowance
for speaking in character. A king might very well suppose
that a wet sea-boy could sleep like a dormouse on the mast-
head during a storm, and a king suffering from insomnia
would be all the more inclined to take this view, but that
was not to say that Shakespeare thought so himself. By my
father's reading of the incident, the young sailor had gone,
or been taken, to St. Paul's like any other of the candidates,
only he had not been sufficiently prepared — prepared for
the length of the service. A call of nature had been too
strong for him; he had gone out to find a public convenience and then felt too self-conscious to come in again. I
considered both these theories ingenious but wrong. In my
view, the young sailor decided that he did not care about
being confirmed, and had the courage of his opinions.

I did not add, for it is no use going into that sort of thing
with even the most emancipated parents (and mine were remarkably emancipated from the usual parental duty to
quell their child), that the young sailor's action had filled
me with such admiration for his independent mind and
such shame at my own sheepish conformity that though I
went on being confirmed, I was to all intents and purposes
unconscious of it. One can never know beforehand what
isn't going to happen to one, or, as a hymn expresses it,
'Sometimes a light surprises the Christian while he sings.' A
light had surprised me. A dove had descended where I was
least expecting it. A profound spiritual experience had

taken place — though a little prematurely — during my confirmation. And by the time my mother had produced my
hat from a paper bag and we were lunching very late in a
City restaurant, I knew that I would follow the young sailor
out.

The Golden Rose

LONG, long ago, when there was a Tzar in Russia, and scarcely an automobile or a divorced person in Mayfair, and when the throne of England was embellished not only by a beautiful queen but by several beautiful mistresses, too, and when rock gardens were still a rarity, and my mother's greatest ambition was to have a black velvet dress with white lace on it, Miss Viner would come to tea.

Miss Viner was a small, wiry woman, with a sharp nose and a voice like a fox terrier—but a very cultured fox terrier, who had learned to yap with dignity. When she arrived, I was sent out of the room. If I put my ear to the door, I used to hear sounds of a nature most unusual in our house—sounds indeed, that seemed almost indissociable from a visit by Miss Viner. I used to hear my mother taking quite a minor part in the conversation. She would listen for as long as five minutes at a time, only interrupting to say, 'Do go on!' or 'And what happened then?' or 'I have sometimes suspected that myself' or 'How tragic for the Empress!' All this was because Miss Viner travelled so extensively in Eastern Europe.

Why she travelled, and how she travelled, we did not know. Sometimes my mother, thinking Miss Viner over, would begin to wonder if Miss Viner were not a secret agent for the British government. For otherwise, said my mother, how could she get to know all these things, and speak so many Balkan languages, and meet so many diplomats, and stay in such grand hotels? And when Miss Viner, after a month or two in Middlesex, shut up her semi-detached residence called Aboukir and went off for another trip through those Balkans, my mother would fall pensive and say, 'One of these days, *she mayn't come back*.'

Though I was sent out of the room when Miss Viner called, my mother shared with me, very generously, the latest news from Eastern Europe. For it was not so much that she feared for the effect of Miss Viner's stories on my innocence as for the possible effect of my innocence on Miss Viner's stories. Eastern Europe, it seemed, was packed with influential queens. There was Marie of Rumania, who wore her hair down her back, and the Empress Elizabeth of Austria—she had worn her hair down her back, too—and Queen Draga of Serbia, who had been murdered, and the Queen of Montenegro, who made such wonderful matches for her daughters. All these queens were immensely powerful and had quantities of pearls. Besides the queens, there were the morganatic consorts. For a morganatic marriage, my mother explained, was really quite correct in Eastern Europe, nothing to be narrow-minded about. Even ladies not morganatically attached to a throne might nevertheless be a very respectable power behind it. It was different in England, where our monarchs married for love.

Miss Viner's most esteemed morganatic was the Countess Sophie Chotek, the non-royal wife of the Archduke Francis Ferdinand of Austria. It was not, reported Miss Viner, that the woman was beautiful. On the contrary, she was plain. But she was intelligent, fascinating, and had the politics of Eastern Europe at her fingers' ends.

Insensibly, I began to picture the Countess Sophie Chotek as being a pretty close likeness of Miss Viner, except that she wore a small diamond coronet and a floating veil, whereas Miss Viner's veil was almost tailor-made, it fitted so closely to her profile and her toque.

And the Countess could twist the Pope, Miss Viner said, round her little finger. In spite of the morganatic marriage, no woman was more warmly received at the Vatican—of course, like so many plain women, she looked her best in black. 'One wears black, you know, when received at the Vatican.' My mother nodded. She knew.

It was through maternal devotion that the Countess twisted the Pope. 'That woman will move Europe,' said Miss Viner, 'mark my words, to get her children recognized as legitimate. And she'll do it, too. The hand of steel in the velvet glove.' I found this odd. I was legitimate, but I never heard my mother rejoicing in it. However, she was heart and soul with the Countess.

During Miss Viner's next absence, my mother kept a sharp eye on the Pope's health, and when Miss Viner returned, my mother's first question concerned the success of the Countess Sophie's efforts.

'My dear, the woman's done it.' These, said my mother, were Miss Viner's very words, for it was remarkable how freely she spoke of these crowned and coroneted heads in Eastern Europe. 'The Pope has sent her the Golden Rose. Privately, of course. But it can only mean one thing.' The Golden Rose, she explained, was an imitation rosebush made of gold, in the branches of which nestled a vial of scented oil, and was a gift which the Holy Father now and again bestowed upon high female dignitaries as a token of his favour.

My mother, repeating these words, 'the Golden Rose,' fell into a rich, musing silence. Presently she got up with decision and walked to her writing table. There she mused some more; then she began to sketch out elevations for sleeve and skirt draperies.

'I have got an idea for my new dinner dress,' she said. 'I have decided on black.'

'With lace?' said I.

'No. With a yellow, with a *deep* yellow rose on the bodice.'

Miss Viner, also collaborating with the Countess, had expressed herself rather differently. On her dressing table at Aboukir, so my mother reported, was a large photograph of the Pope. She had chosen, as it turned out, the more durable love token, for in a month or two Edward VII died, and my mother, mourning loyally, removed the yellow rose from her dinner dress.

Very shortly Miss Viner went off again, in her mysterious way, this time to Russia. Her unfurred return was a considerable disappointment to my mother; there was not as much as a sable tail on her. Her stories, too, were of quite a new kind. Shaken out of her usual lofty diction, she yapped as passionately as a fox terrier that has met a rat—a large rat. In Russia, it seemed, Miss Viner's blood had alternately boiled and frozen. And she poured out a jangling account of police spies, and typhus, and censorship, and terrorism, and corruption—a coil of horrors amid which even Miss Viner, so imperturbable, knowing so much about Eastern Europe, and acquainted with so many diplomats, walked in fear.

'And the Tzar,' inquired my mother, 'and the Tzarina, poor thing? And all those Grand Dukes and Grand Duchesses?'

'Miserable puppets!' answered Miss Viner, with a toss of her toque.

My mother tried to lure her into the sunnier parts of Eastern Europe, tactfully remarking that she had never really wanted to see St. Petersburg; Vienna was more to her fancy. But it was not much use. Even after the second cup of tea, Miss Viner was still brooding around the fortress of Saints Peter and Paul. Russia had unsettled her—unsettled her to such an extent that soon afterwards she gave up the lease of Aboukir and came to tea no longer.

She was a great loss. For a long while we remembered her and her stories. The details of Balkan politics got a little dim, but the pearls remained as lustrous as ever. When the Countess Sophie Chotek was shot in the streets of Sarajevo on June 28th, 1914, I saw my mother shake her head, sagely and sorrowfully, and guessed she was thinking how little even the Golden Rose had availed that skilful lady.

As for Miss Viner, it was years before I saw her again. It was soon after the war; Eastern Europe had been considerably remodelled; and as for me, I was sitting in a teashop thinking about Freud, as one often did at that period, when I heard a familiar fox terrier's voice remarking, 'Of course, one of the Grand Duchesses is at this moment in Chicago.'

I looked round. There was Miss Viner, neat and erect as ever, scarcely aged at all, complying not so much with Time as with Progress, for she was heavily and inefficiently made up. Her companion was a stoutish, red-haired woman, younger than she, who seemed less interested in Miss Viner than in a dish of fancy pastries.

'But she has completely lost her memory.'

'You can't really wonder at that, considering what she's been through,' said the red-haired woman philosophically. And with an expression of well-rounded resolve she helped herself to a cream horn. Presently she asked, her glance again perambulating the dish of cakes, 'How did you do on your last trip? Business good?'

'Disgusting,' replied Miss Viner. 'Slack as can be. And the hotels! You should have seen it in the old days.'

This time the red-haired woman chose a macaroon.

'If you ask me,' she said, 'you made your mistake staying on with the old firm. You'd have done better if you'd gone in for something more up-to-date, even if it meant a smaller commission. Nobody wants those old-fashioned transformations nowadays.'

Stanley Sherwood,

OR THE FIREMAN'S REVENGE

CHANGE of climate will do much. It will change a negligible herb into an overwhelming weed, or a weed into a greenhouse rarity. It does things to rabbits, too. We all know about those rabbits in Australia, though I, for one, have a rather confused recollection of the sequence of events. Clover was imported, and then humblebees to fertilize the clover, and when the humblebees got above themselves the rabbits were brought to discourage the humblebees — something retributory and Marxian of that sort. Anyhow, it ended in the rabbits being a menace to Australia.

Another variety of animate life affected by climate is butlers. When I visited New York at the turn of the decade, I met a great quantity of English butlers who had been imported, I understood, to combat prohibition, as the rabbits were imported to combat the humblebees; and I was interested to observe how they were reacting to climatic changes. I noticed, for instance, that they showed a strong tendency to be called William, whereas in England butlers are never called William. Jeeves, or Thompson, or even Williams. But not William. Another thing that I noticed about the English butlers in New York was the remarkable amelioration in their dispositions. Either the climate or combating prohibition had brought out all that was genial in their characters. They seemed a new and kindlier race. I could not reconcile them with the English butlers I had known in England. Particularly, I could not reconcile them with my mother's butler.

My mother's butler was named Stanley Sherwood. He was

a slender, sallow man. His expression was at once ravenous and demure; he had a profile as accurate as though it had been snipped out of a piece of paper; his tread was noiseless; he had a tendency to fold his hands. His memory was as accurate as his profile, he was punctual to the minute, he never forgot a duty or a commission; his clothes were always brushed, his demeanour was always correct. He was like some baleful drug, which, once you have imbibed it, you cannot do without. My father referred to him as Ignatius Loyola.

This loathsome character and impeccable butler was, of course, quite as much my father's butler as my mother's butler. But we looked on him as my mother's butler. She had always wanted a butler and a chinchilla muff, and in one year, in a sudden access of prosperity, she received them both. As for the chinchilla muff, she has portions of it yet; when I saw it last, it was ornamenting a negligee. Not a shred of Stanley Sherwood is preserved in the family, I am glad to say.

But for many years it seemed as though Stanley Sherwood would be forever with us. It was impossible to catch him in fault, for he was faultless; so we could not dismiss him. Nor would he leave us; for though it was clear that he disliked and despised us, the man had such a revoltingly cool and tolerant disposition that it was impossible to provoke him into giving his notice. Death would not take pity on our sufferings—Stanley Sherwood was never ill. Unlike the chinchilla muff, he could not be stolen or mislaid, and no moth would have looked at him; he was far too innutritious.

It was the incident of the boiler which made my father call Sherwood Ignatius Loyola. One winter's evening, my father was writing when Sherwood appeared at his elbow, erect, noiseless, sinister, like the serpent appearing to Eve. My father was in the middle of a paragraph. He said, 'One moment, Sherwood.' It was quite a long moment, during which my father finished his paragraph, and read it through, and titivated it. When he was finally satisfied that it was the sort of paragraph he had meant it to be, he said,

'Well, Sherwood?' Sherwood said, 'If you please, sir, the boiler has burst.' By then the house was flooded and ruin was spread abroad. But no one could say it was Sherwood's fault.

I have never known any human being with such icy breath as Sherwood's. Ladies dining with us used to shudder as blasts from Sherwood played across their naked shoulders; bald-headed colonels, enjoying my mother's peculiarly Bengal curries, used to start and flinch aside. But Sherwood's breath was cold not only physically but spiritually. There was a disdainful asceticism about Sherwood's breath; it was as though those gales blew from some moral Arctic. On one occasion he added a touch all of his own to this general effect of *memento mori*. Wine, in our house, was offered under the simple choice of 'red or white wine'. Sherwood had been offering, in his usual stealthy undertones, red or white wine for years. Suddenly, secretively, Sherwood became aware of the French language. And we heard him going round the table saying, on his icy breath, 'Bone or Graves.'

It came as a great surprise to us to learn that Sherwood could smile, for we had never seen a smile on his face. It was my mother's aunt who taught us better; a woman of candour, she observed on one of her visits, 'Nora, I cannot endure the way your Sherwood smiles.' Recovering from her first impulse of incredulity, my mother went into the matter further, and discovered that when Sherwood opened the front door to my great-aunt he smiled at her — 'a ghastly smile,' my great-aunt said.

We could well believe it was ghastly. My mother became agitated. It was questionable etiquette for any butler to smile at visitors, and certainly Sherwood was not adapted for smiling. She began to make inquiries of her friends. She could not bring herself to ask outright. 'Does my butler smile at you?' It is a difficult question to ask. She went around it with discreet questionings, indirect approaches. 'I cannot imagine Sherwood smiling, can you?' or 'Do tell me, candidly, is there anything unusual about the look of the hall when the door is first opened?' or 'I often wonder what impression this house makes on strangers.' The replies were equally discreet, equally impersonal. But for all that, my mother received an impression that something was being kept from her.

She decided to learn the worst. Ordinarily, she let herself into the house with a latchkey. This afternoon, however, she rang the front-door bell. The door opened with exemplary promptitude. Even in her anxiety, my mother could not help admiring the noiseless speed with which Sherwood rose from his pantry in the basement as genies rise from lamps at the word of command. The door opened, and there was Sherwood, sallow, slender, well-brushed. But as the door opened, his jaws opened too. Sherwood smiled. My great-aunt had been quite right. Sherwood's smile was ghastly.

'Sherwood!' exclaimed my mother impetuously. 'Don't smile like that.'

'Very good, Madam,' said Sherwood, the smile vanishing like a fairy at sunrise.

My mother is a very conscientious woman; when she gives her mind to anything, she does it thoroughly. It now seemed to her that one prohibition might not be enough to clear Sherwood's countenance of smiles.

'I shall ring the bell once more,' she said. 'And you must let me in without smiling. I want to be sure that you —' *Never smile again* was the phrase that came naturally, but she concluded, 'get out of this bad habit.'

Sherwood said, 'Very good, Madam,' and closed the door. Again my mother rang, again the door was opened. Again that ghastly smile flickered on Sherwood's lank chops. My mother said it would not do and was again shut out.

The fourth time the door opened, the smile was sickly as well as ghastly. Remembering that things are darkest before dawn, my mother encouraged Sherwood to control himself and told him to try again. These kind words did no good at all. The fifth and sixth time that Sherwood opened the door to my mother he was, she said, gnashing his teeth at her.

On the seventh opening, Sherwood panted but did not smile. If my mother had been advised, she would have left well alone, but her conscientiousness was too much for her. She must needs make a good job of it.

'Once more, Sherwood,' she said, encouragingly, 'just to be sure that it's all right.'

'Very good, Madam.'

The smile was back again, and verging on a leer.

It occurred to my mother to work on Sherwood by force of example.

'This time,' she said, 'you will ring the bell, and I will open the door.'

Sherwood rang the bell. My mother, wearing a look of glacial calm, opened the door. 'Like that,' she said. 'Now you do it.'

But the door was opened by a smiling Sherwood.

By now there was quite a crowd gathered on the opposite side of the street, watching these strange performances on the Warners' doorstep. My mother entered her home with a sigh, saying, 'Tomorrow we will try again.'

That night, tossing on her fevered bed, snatching a few minutes' sleep, my mother dreamed that Sherwood, wearing black kid gloves and a necklace of tiger's teeth, gave notice. She woke, and thought it very likely, and rejoiced, and fell asleep again and dreamed that Sherwood was murdering her. This seemed likely, too. We had always surmised that our Ignatius Loyola had violent passions, however sternly concealed.

'I must try again,' she said to my father the next morning. 'It would be fatal to give way.' My father said, 'Why not practise at the garden door?' My mother said that it was a base and unworthy expedient, but acted on his advice. By the end of the week, she reported that Sherwood scarcely smiled at all, and we took her word for it and left it at that.

So did Sherwood, though for some weeks we palpitated with the fond idea that rancour was slowly boiling up in him and might explode in an announcement of his departure. We had often prayed to death to take away our Sherwood, but it was love, strong as death, that freed us in the end. We had a thin, grim housemaid, and to our astonishment and rapture Sherwood got her with child. Smiling on the fault, my mother dismissed them both, and promised to be godmother.

Sherwood remained in the town; he opened a sweetshop and enrolled himself as one of the town fire brigade. As fireman, he wore a glittering brass helmet much too large for him and looked, so my mother said, like a weevil in a nut. She also compared him, flashing by on the fire engine, to the Rider on the Pale Horse in the Book of Revelations.

For a long while we took pains not to catch fire, but in the end grew careless, and one evening a neighbour rang up to say that flames were coming from our chimney stack. I was out at the moment, but heard the whole story half an hour later when I came in. My mother summoned the fire brigade. They came, led by Sherwood. Under the helmet his eyes, she said, had a baleful glare, and he fingered the axe at his belt. She wished with all her heart that my father were not dead. She even wished that I were not out. But concealing her disquiet, she advised Sherwood to look for the fire on the roof. The ladder was set up; she heard Sherwood go clanking upwards, followed by his mates. Then there were some shouts and tramplings, and the mates came down again, saying that it was all right now. 'Where is Sherwood?' she asked. They said he would be down in a minute, he was just having a last look around.

'At that very instant,' said my mother to me, 'there was a rumble and a thud, and a stink of soot, and shrieks from the kitchen, and Dora and Mary shot up the kitchen stairs in strong hysterics, covered with soot and chemicals. I knew in a flash what Sherwood had done. Lurking about on our roof like that, snuffing down the chimney pots, he had made sure which was the kitchen chimney. And then he launched down the jet from one of his infernal machines.'

'A fire extinguisher?' I suggested.

'I said infernal machine, didn't I? And Dora and Mary and the dinner and the kitchen are all one mass of soot and bicarbonate of soda, or whatever the loathsome chemical is. And the kitchen fire is out. And God only knows when we shall eat a cooked meal again.'

'Did he smile at parting?' I asked.

'You couldn't call it a smile,' said my mother. 'But he was just faintly licking his lips.'

Shadows of Death

SUNDAY after Sunday when I was a child I used to contemplate the Seven Cardinal Virtues in a stained-glass window, and weigh the sartorial advantages of being Hope in green, Temperance in strawberry pink, or Justice in a splendid shade of purple. Fortitude was out of the running, for I knew I should never be allowed to wear armour. But Faith, Hope, Charity, Justice, Temperance, and Prudence had each much to be said for them; and might have been attainable if poor Ted Hooper had not been stricken with tuberculosis and my clothes, as a consequence, made by Mrs. Hooper, who needed to earn now that her husband could earn no longer.

Everybody in our small society knew Ted Hooper. He was employed by the livery stables, and though there were other drivers he was the star of the establishment, for he drove with such style, and looked so elegant sitting up on the box with his straight back and the jaunty cockade in his hat. Whether one sat in the closed brougham watching the rain spatter against the windows, or airily in the victoria, raised in a temporary splendour above the common lot of those who trudged on foot or sweltered in trains, the presence of Ted Hooper substantiated one's sense of well-being. Ted Hooper was always so smiling and obliging, and considered his horse, and never seemed to mind how long he was kept waiting, conveying the impression that he was not only part of one's pleasure but took a share in it.

'When can I sit on the box beside Ted Hooper?'

'Perhaps when you are a little older.'

And then all of a sudden—for he was in such demand and such a willing servant that he went on driving long after he should have been at home nursing that tiresome cough—he was no longer erect and cockaded in upper air but felled and flattened on a bed, and being spoken of deploringly, and almost as though he were a dead person already.

It was at this juncture that my mother, paying a visit of practical condolence, discovered that Mrs. Hooper smocked.

A smock frock is the long-sleeved, knee-length shirt, made of heavy linen, which generations of English rustics wore as an outer garment. Smocking is the process by which it was rendered approximately rainproof and wind-proof over the shoulders and across the breast and back. The garment was cut enormously wide and then gathered into tiny pleats, which were held in place by a close reticulation of stitches, each stitch securing a pleat and tethering it to its neighbour. The resulting texture is as thick, as stiff, and almost as weatherproof as hide. If Ted Hooper had been dressed in his wife's handiwork, he would have been much better protected against wind and rain than he was in his close-fitting livery jacket of bottle-green cloth—so my mother remarked, adding that this was quite beside the point, since, for one thing, no jobmaster would employ a driver who wore a smock frock; for another, no one nowadays would be seen dead in such an old-fashioned affair.

The latter did not apply to my mother's daughter.

My smocked frocks were sturdy enough—that I grate-fully admitted; I daresay they looked rather pretty; they helped Mrs. Hooper; they may even have helped to preserve a discarded traditional skill. But there was a depressing sameness about them, a too classical uniformity. I wore brown holland smocks for everyday, white linen smocks for Sundays, blue serge with scarlet smocking for winter. Patterned materials were ruled out by my mother. How foolish a field labourer would have looked following the plough in a patterned smock! And though I went to my dancing class in grass-green or rose-coloured silk, I was still smocked around my top and my wrists, and elsewhere totally ungarnished. Envy consumed me when Nina Barnett, bounding at my side in the *pas de Basque*, unfurled her accordion-pleated satin, when Marjorie Watkins fluttered her rosebud-patterned chiffon as she hauled at the invisible rope in the hornpipe — envy that I tried to smother under snobbery, quite as base a passion, since, after begging in vain for rosebuds and accordion pleating, I had been made aware by my mother that Nina and Marjorie lived on the other side of the hill, and with the sort of mothers who overdressed everything, from daughters to puddings, which no doubt they called sweets.

Nor was smocking all. My mother soon found out that Mrs. Hooper, repository of traditional arts, knew how to make sun-bonnets.

'You can come with me to Maidments, and help me choose some pretty patterns.'

Even the very moderate degree of pattern my mother allowed me to help her choose — a lilac sprig, a blue dot — made sun-bonnets a thrilling prospect. But when it came to wearing the things, no wealth of arabesque, no flaunt of colour, no riot of rose garlands from the other side of the hill could have reconciled me to being at once blinkered, deafened, and half cooked. Fortunately, sun-bonnets could be disposed of. When I had dropped one in a horse-pond, used another to carry mulberries in, and left two or three in trees, no more were ordered from Mrs. Hooper.

Mrs. Hooper, as I now realize, must have thought all this smocking and sun-bonneting an extreme example of gentry dementia. Making conversation to Ted — and those who tend a drawn-out dying have to make a great deal of conversation — she must often have remarked that she could not understand it, really she could not, a lady who wore such pretty clothes herself insisting on these old

110

bygones for her little girl, more like a charity child than anything else, and paying as much for them as if they had been something dainty with lace. Why, even when she was a girl, smocks and sun-bonnets had gone to the scarecrows, and she had only learned how to make them because Great-Aunt Hetty had promised her the tea set. . . . Mrs. Hooper was too gentle for scorn, but there was certainly a note of puzzled commiseration in her assurances, as the latest specimen was tried on and the cuirass of smocking patted into place, that it looked very sweet, it did really, very sweet and quite quaint.

Since Ted could not be left, in case another bleeding should come on, these assurances were spoken in the flat above the stables where Ted's employers allowed him to live on. The stables were about half a mile's walk away from our house—long enough for a sense of ceremonial and adventure to accumulate. There was a man-size door cut in the tall green carriage gates, and inside was the cobbled yard, the smell of horse dung, the smell of hay, the old watchdog waking and wandering stiffly out of his kennel, the sound of a horse munching, the sound of Ted coughing overhead. It now seems to me that these walks were always undertaken latish on summer afternoons, when the yard had been freshly sluiced and the sun pouring in through the west-facing windows filled the low rooms with an acuteness of colour, an intensity of habitation that our rooms at home never had. The door opening from the sitting-room to the bedroom was kept on the jar. When I was taken by my nurse, I was shepherded away from it. But if my mother had taken me, she would say, after a glance of inquiry and an assenting nod, 'Now go in and say how-do-you-do to Mr. Hooper.'

He lay propped up in a brass bed, and on the walls were photographs of relations, horses, Queen Victoria, and a village church smothered in ivy. There was a queer gay look about him, an insubstantial festiveness. His cheeks were as brightly and patchily pink as if he were a painted wooden toy, his dark eyes glittered, he seemed to be having

111

a private party alone with the photographs and the streaking light — a party for which he had put on his best nightshirt. But his hands belied the rest. They were too large, too real, to join in the party, and when they crooked themselves round his spitting bowl, there was something sad and awkward and servile in the gesture.

A few years later when my grandfather lay dying of the same disease, I was not allowed into his room, and made my how-do-you-dos from the passage. In his case, there was no call for the etiquette of good manners that obtained in visiting the poor.

When I was young, it was part of one's education to learn how to make such visits befittingly, what questions to ask, what gifts to take and how to give them without offending. My mother did such things admirably, though she took no pleasure in them and certainly never felt any mitigating glows of goodness. On the contrary, once out of the house and round the corner, she would hurry to wash off any stains of virtue by going to the pastry cook's for a cup of coffee and a macaroon, or to the nursery garden to buy another fuchsia, or poke about in the second-hand-furniture shop. Her ministrations were exclusively practical; if she could have bestowed them on a mangy old dog or a deserving donkey (but, indeed, she often did) she would have found a great deal more fulfilment in them; and she always put on a flippant hat for such occasions, in order not to look like a 'Goodie.' ('Goodies' were ladies who visited their complemental 'Poories' with an eye to being religiously improving and improved.) So, though I was almost seventeen when our leading Goodie, then nearing another lying-in, asked me to take over visiting Mrs. Darwin, who had cancer, I had had no practise in supplying spiritual consolations. But such, I knew, would be expected of me, since this was indeed a leading Goodie, one born in the episcopal purple, and a great-niece of Mr. Gladstone's, enthusiastically pious and convinced that all and sundry only needed an ardent shove in the right direction to become pious, too.

'I'm sure you know Mrs. Darwin. She's such a dear person!'

I knew Mrs. Darwin's cakes, and that Mr. Darwin's opinion on hotbeds was much valued by our gardener, so I agreed that I knew Mrs. Darwin.

'There's no hope for her, I'm afraid. But she has so enjoyed our little quiet readings. Can you manage Tuesday afternoons?'

'What book have you been reading? I expect she would like me to go on with it.'

'Oh, *The Imitation of Christ*. One can't do better.'

Pleased to oblige in any measure, I said with alacrity, 'We've got a copy of that, I know.'

This was not a success. I have since found that assents made with alacrity seldom are, when made to Goodies. They prefer one to sound as if the road would wind uphill all the way, and the shirt be hairy.

I hastened to add, 'Where did you leave off?'

The Goodie flushed. It was plain she did not remember where. As though brushing off a fly in a Christian spirit, she said, 'Any chapter will do, I imagine.' So this was not much of a success, either. I realized I still had something to learn.

I told my mother none of this. (I suppose it was a time when we were having one of our quarrels and civilly ignoring each other's goings on.) I remember wishing, though, when Tuesday came, that it had been winter, when I could have put *The Imitation of Christ* into a muff. It was midsummer, brilliantly hot and fine, the sort of weather when, if you have to lie in bed, it is impossible to pretend that you are doing so from choice. My feelings when I set out were inconveniently positive. I was afraid of what I might find, I was embarrassed to be thrusting myself on someone I did not know, I was pretty sure I was about to be a hypocrite. As I went into Mrs. Darwin's bedroom, all this was abolished by the superior positiveness of a person who is under sentence of death and still remains alive. A canary burst into song. Mrs. Darwin said he liked visitors; the canary led to Mrs. Pring's parrot, an esteemed mutual acquaintance; a potted geranium opened into Mr. Darwin's prospects for the flower show. It could have seemed like any other pleasant trivial conversation on a fine summer afternoon if there had not been, when she spoke or replied, a quality of belatedness, such as an echo, answering from a distance, has. But a sense of duty reminded me that I was there not to talk about thunderstorms and vegetable marrows but to read aloud from a celebrated manual of devotion. I opened the book. Mrs. Darwin closed her eyes. I suppose few people could open *The Imitation of Christ* for the first time and fail to be charmed by its simplicity, its candour, its gentle sotto-voce insistence — a tune that Augustan poets heard in brooks and described as 'purling.' I turned a page, it purled on, I turned another page. . . . I could understand why people who read it aloud to sufferers found it soothing. A sensation of being soothed was slightly overcoming me, too, and the canary had fallen silent, tweaking his bosom for lice but without much conviction. Mrs. Darwin shifted in her bed and muttered at her pain. She would die, we would all die, centuries would be turned like pages; but Thomas à Kempis would continue to purl, a brook that would never reach an ocean. But then, again, why shouldn't he? Nuns are contented with their narrow cells, Wordsworth contentedly occupied himself in writing the sonnets to the River Duddon — though fortunately he wrote other things as well. . . .

After reading for fifteen minutes, I shut up *The Imitation of Christ* — I'm afraid with a slight bang. Mrs. Darwin lay with closed eyes. Her forehead was flushed; there was sweat on her upper lip. The woman who remained alive had been almost entirely usurped by the woman under sentence of death. When she opened her eyes, the beauty of those pure lucent grey irises was so astonishing, and her eyes were so like something immortal and detached negligently inhabiting a body it had nothing in common with, that I was stricken to the heart and

114

prepared to go on with Thomas à Kempis till nightfall, if Mrs. Darwin wished it.

'Thank you very much.'

Since it seemed that she did not wish it, I said that I must be going, that I hoped I had not stayed too long and overtired her.

'It is very kind of you to come, I'm sure,' she said, making no attempt to delay me.

'And may I come next Tuesday?'

'That would be very nice.'

'And then we could go on with the reading. Unless there is something else you would like better?'

She looked me up and down, thoughtfully, discreetly. Apparently the scrutiny satisfied her, for the woman who had remained alive re-emerged, and gave me a very kindly smile. 'Well—to tell the truth—' She paused for another glance, but it was a brief one. 'To tell the truth, I've always been fond of a nice novel.'

I said that I really did not see why we should let a whole week go by, and it was agreed that I should come the day after tomorrow.

What happened next I can only attribute to the intervention of the Holy Ghost, since of myself—in the words of the catechism—I was not able to do this thing. If it had not been for such an intervention, I do not see how Mrs. Darwin could have been preserved from one of the nice novels of Dostoevski, unless by falling into the cat's-cradle mercies of the latest Henry James. As it was, when I got home I went straight to the spare-room bookcase, whence, after having replaced *The Imitation of Christ*, I removed *The City of Beautiful Nonsense*, by Ernest Temple Thurston, *The Visits of Elizabeth*, by Elinor Glyn, and *Peter's Mother*, by Mrs. de la Pasture.

A Winding Stair, a Fox Hunt, a Fulfilling Situation, Some Sycamores, and the Church at Henning

ENGLISH people don't visit country churches now as they used to when I was young. This is partly because modern cars are so difficult to stop. By the time one has finished saying, 'There's a church. Why don't we have a look at it?' the car has gone on past recall. Even if one sees the church some miles before one draws level with it, and the driver's mind is sufficiently disengaged to hear what one's saying, it takes so long to park the car and to lock the steering and the doors and then to have second thoughts about tractors coming round the corner and to unlock the doors and the steering and find a new place that would have been perfect if there hadn't been a pond there, or a motor bicycle, that one is lucky if one ascertains more about the church's inside than its temperature, if it is winter, and the fact, at all times of year, that it has a font.

When I was young, cars were more amenable. You stopped, got out, and left them; if you were humane and it was, again, winter, you threw a rug over the bonnet. Then you spent half an hour or so investigating the church, reading its mural tablets and drawing conclusions on the character of its incumbent from the state of things in the vestry. And when you saw the car again, it was sitting where you left it, unharmed and undisputed, and the rug was in the ditch. But it isn't only this business of cars. When I was young, visiting village churches was fashionable. Intellectuals practised it as a form of Conspicuous Waste. Later on, some even took to going to church. This always struck me as *outré*. One can carry a fashion too far.

116

Fashion has veered. Though I know several people half my age who find it quite easy to stop their cars outside, they go in for different motives. They are specialists. They have heard that the north transept contains a baroque monument or that the organ has some remains of Father Smith. They haven't the same broadminded passion that carried me into every country church I could lay foot in, when I was young.

It was a passion that made demands. For one thing, I hadn't got a car. For another, I hadn't got a husband or a dear old Scotch nanny or anything of that sort which I could leave William with. William was my black chow dog. William and I pursued our churches on foot, as nearly as the crow flies as bridle paths and cuts across fields would allow. William sported free as air; I carried William's lead and harness and a large-scale ordnance map. When we approached the church's village, William was harnessed and led. Harnessed and led, he accompanied me round the outside of the church, looking increasingly indifferent. He knew what would happen next. His lead would be tied to a railing, or looped round some convenient crocket, and he would be left to meditation and philosophy. This was not unkind. Usually he was quite glad to sit down and bite burrs off his paws. On this particular occasion, I tethered him to a holy door scraper and in a southern aspect just outside the porch.

The church was even larger than it had looked from a distance. (This, I may say, doesn't happen except with churches that are really large; ordinary-sized churches dwindle.) As I walked about in it, I was continually looking up at the roof, and wishing I had the moral courage to shout—the echo would have been so rewarding. Eight furry bell ropes hung in the space beneath the tower. When I tried the door into the tower stairway and found it wasn't locked, I was not, however, so spontaneously pleased as I should have been. It was a corkscrew stair, and the steps were steep and irregular. Saying to myself that I could always turn back if I didn't like it—or for that matter come down backwards, a method that has much to be said for it—I started to go up. There was light ahead from a window, which I presently found coincided with a landing and the door into the ringing chamber. Here were the furry ropes again, but smoother with handling. Ringing charts were nailed to the wall, and on some of them were dates and boasts: '27th July 1904. 2½ hours,' and so on. I thought of those eight sweating men, conjoined by pattern-keeping into one man; and how dizzily, after the last of the changes, the conjoined man must have come to pieces, each looking round on his fellows and shaking down into his mere singleness again. From here on, the stairs were steeper but not so worn, being less often used; and, thinking of campanology and by now grown into the rhythm of circling round and round the newels, I got up them pretty cleverly. The window on the second landing was louvred. I heard the wind flirting in it as I went upwards, and felt the cold of upper air. The bell-chamber door was bolted, but I drew the bolt and looked in. There they were, the eight of them, roosting like enormous doves in their nest of machinery. I rubbed the rim of the nearest, and presently it began to whine. They were the heart and reason of the tower, I thought; and now I might go down. The stair wound on into darkness. I groped up and up, pawing my way, and at last a drizzle of light fell on me, sifting round the edge of the flap door. It opened more easily than I expected. The rush of light almost knocked me downstairs. Holding my ordnance map between my teeth I squirmed myself on to the leads, where the first thing I saw was a cigarette carton and the next a trouser button.

The next thing I saw was the roof of the nave, which from the ground level had seemed so immensely high and from here was so far below me that I might have been looking down at a cat on the hearthrug.

I spread my map on the parapet and began to study the bright October landscape of pasture and woodland and honey-coloured plough. There, so close, was the larch wood I had skirted round. There, so flattened, was the rise of ground from which I had first got my view of the church. There, were farmsteads, roads, villages, solitary elms and elm avenues like veins of metal. There, was a white-faced Georgian house in its park, looking like a sheep. There, was Brent Goodleigh, and Snuffham, and Darcy Cantelo and Darcy All Saints. There, was the railway, with a train on it, methodical as a caterpillar.

I moved my map to the southern parapet. Just flowing into view was a fox hunt. At this remove, whence I could not see the fox enjoying the sport nor the purple faces of the riders who were so arduously procuring him his fun, it was an animating spectacle. The hounds looked clean and the autumn-coloured horses suited the landscape. If they had been pursuing the M.F.H. it would have been wholly delightful. I glanced down at William. He was asleep. I identified a couple more villages. By then the hounds, who hadn't been running with much conviction, had gone into a little wood, where they stood about like a chorus of Druids in 'Norma'. I was just moving round to the eastern parapet when I heard William barking. He was barking at a clergyman; and as the clergyman was hatless I thought it probable that he was the church's own clergyman, who wished to enter his own church. 'William!' I shouted, hoping the clergyman wasn't also called William. There was the clergyman, sometimes making a discreet step towards the porch and then rescinding it. There was William, ramping like a lion, straining at his leash and barking quite horribly. And there was I on top of the tower and quite unable to do anything about either of them. 'William!' I shouted again. After several shouts, the clergyman looked up. Naturally, he would be more expectant than William of voices from heaven. He looked up. I looked down. It was a first step, but it didn't take us very far. Meanwhile William was hurling himself towards the interloper more violently than ever, and I expected at any moment to see the door scraper torn from its foundations. Then I remembered that there was a little door into the chancel (such doors are called priest's doors) and that it was open — for I had gone out by it to warm myself in the sun. I gestured to the clergyman. He stepped back, to see my gesture more clearly. William considered he was routed, and left off barking. Snatching at this moment of silence, I cupped my voice in my hands and shouted briefly, 'Go round to the other door.' I thought this showed generalship and presence of mind. But when I had closed the flap door on myself and was scrambling down those interminable steps, I also thought it had sounded as if I were expecting the clergyman to deliver groceries.

I was down at last. The church was ringing with silence, and there was the clergyman.

'My awful dog —'

'I waited to see you safely down.'

We mingled our apologies, I for my dog, he for his stairs. He was a most amiable man — I still cannot imagine why William took against him — and in no time the apologies turned into admirations, his for my handsome animal, mine for his splendid church. He showed me round it, and before I left he unlocked the safe to show me the registers, which went back to 1618. If there was any umbrage in his heart at having been addressed as though he were the groceries, he did not show it. Perhaps all that spiral jolting had given my conscience a morbid turn, and really there was nothing to fret about in what was a happy and fulfilling situation. He, bemused by William's barkings, had been in a fix; I had directed him out of it. The laity must play its part.

The last village I identified before William's barks narrowed my horizon was called Henning. I had time to observe that its church lay quite apart from the village — usually a sign of an old structure — and was approached by an avenue. But what with one thing and another, I did not approach it till July of the following year.

Its avenue was of sycamores — a tree which I respect (the

120

Greek Anthology calls it 'thick-tressed') but prefer in
clumps. These sycamores had been planted too close
together, and were decaying for lack of attention.
Sycamore leaves, too, hold a great deal of water, and
though by the time I walked the avenue it was no longer
raining, raindrops continued to plop and patter through
them. William walked sombrely beside me. I tied him to a
railing and assured him I should not be long. With the
best will in the world to be pleased with Henning, now that
I saw it I didn't expect a great deal from it. It had a high-
shouldered, asthmatic appearance, but wasn't tall enough
to warrant its clerestory windows, and there was a dead
blackbird in the porch.

I stopped in the porch to read the notices. The
preponderance of them had to do with missions: missions
to Africa, to India, to seamen; a missionary meeting with
lantern slides; a Sale of work for the Church Mission
Society. One must not hold a fabric responsible for the
type of notices pinned in its porch; for all that, my
prejudice deepened. This church, I thought, is taking too
much on itself. Such busybody insistence on spreading the
Gospel is all of a piece with those uncalled-for clerestory
windows.

I opened the door and leaped in. The leap was forced on
me: the floor of the church was a deep step below the level
of the porch, and I had not noticed this in time. If, instead
of drawing my attention to the needs of such large portions of
the globe, the incumbent had allowed charity to begin
at home with a notice of 'Mind the Step' . . . My
resentment flickered out: he could not have afforded the
pasteboard, the unwatered ink. I had never seen a church
so ground down into poverty. In a disheartened way, it was
clean—fairly clean. The woodwork was rubbed; but no
polish had been afforded. The floor was swept; but it
would have taken more than a broom, it would have taken
ten strong women with gallons of boiling water and cartons
of yellow soap, to get the grime of long damp out of the
flagged floor. There was a leak in the roof of the

121

chancel—a white bedroom basin had been put on the altar to catch the drips. Through the clerestory windows the light glared in and itemized every stain, fray, fading, deficiency, poor makeshift. And when I looked about for a collecting box that might be labelled 'Fabric' or 'Restoration Fund' or even 'Organ'—for in the vehemence of my compassion I would even have contributed to the organ—I found only boxes dedicated to missions. At which I put my money back again, missions not appealing to me.

I was going away in rage and frustration when, turning back for a last look at that melancholy vista and the sad white bedroom basin, I happened to glance upward. And there I saw the most amazing thing. All round the church, skied between the clerestory windows and the roof, was a frieze of pale animals, modelled in low relief, each animal spaced out and in profile. They were of all kinds, and they were all of the same size. This did not make the elephant seem small. It made the dog behind him seem gigantic. The crocodile opened its jaws to no purpose; they could not possibly enclose the towering rump of the rabbit. As all these animals faced the same way, they appeared to be noiselessly pursuing each other.

And in my hasty arrogance of compassion, I had nearly missed this wonder of wonders!

The noiselessness of their pursuit had so imposed itself on my mind that presently I realized that by comparison the silence of the church was only relative. The intermittent drip from the chancel roof chimed like a very small bell. A fly buzzed. A clock ticked in the vestry. July is a songless month, but favourable to insects. I kept on hearing a faint cloudy murmur, quite unplaceable, which I supposed was a late swarming of bees.

Provided they did not swarm on William . . . Bees are drawn to black—or are they repelled by it? I could not rightly remember. It was one or the other. I went on looking at the animals. A ram, a lion, a hind, a boar, a dog, an elephant, a different kind of dog, possibly a wolf, a cow, a porcupine, a leopard, a monkey, a goat, a crocodile, a rabbit, a bear, an ox, a camel . . . Another drip. By now the basin must be beginning to fill, and before I left it would be a kindly act to empty it in the churchyard. It was a very persistent leak; the rain had been over for a long while. A cow, a porcupine, a leopard, a monkey, a goat, a crocodile, a rabbit, a bear, an ox, a camel, a badger, a sow, a horse, a ram, a lion, a hind, a boar, a dog, an elephant . . . And at some time or other every one of these animals had been food for some kind of man. William had no notion how edible he was: a sailor I met in a train told me he had seen rows of little Williams, about the size of sucking pigs, hung up outside butcher's shops in Canton. Poor William—I had told that innocent edible animal I would not be long.

A magpie chattered. A bee flew in and presently flew out again. A camel, a badger, a sow, a horse, a ram . . . The artist of the Henning animals was as single-minded as any of his beasts. He had no truck with allegory or heraldry or grotesque. He was faithful to his intention, and to his measurements: the rhythm of his spacing kept their pursuit alive. Paperhangers sell friezes of animals for decorating nurseries, and parents buy them and think them delightful and just what children would like. What children think of them I have never been in a position to know, but if such friezes are just what children like, one can reasonably assume that children take a very superficial view of animals. Nothing could be much more ill-suited to catch a parent's or a paperhanger's fancy than these pale Henning creatures, fatalistically pursuing each other through the centuries. I felt assured that in the generations of Henning children there had always been children to whom they were more than a solace through sermons, more than meat and drink, more than parents or wild strawberries or birds nesting—children who, even when they had been hounded out of Eden, still fed their minds on this mysterious plain statement leading to nothing. And on a winter night, a night when everything was rigid with frost and nothing stirred or quickened except the stars flashing overhead, such a child, grown older, would look up farther, and see Ursa and Draco and Lynx silently pursuing each other through the heavens.

A child's mind has more hardihood. For myself, I was becoming increasingly intimidated by these encircling animals. How long I had subjected myself to not being their quarry only the clock in the vestry knew—for at this date I scorned to wear a watch. A cow, a porcupine, a leopard, a monkey . . . Drip. I remembered that I was going to empty that basin before I left. I wandered up to the altar and looked in the basin. It was not more than a quarter full of honey.

My Mother Won the War

I THINK it is pretty generally admitted that my
mother won the last war.* By generally admitted I do
not mean officially recognized. Offical recognition
would have involved many difficulties. Admirals and Field-
Marshals, for instance, who had spent their lives in the
study of warfare, and panted into their sixties towards the
happy day when those studies might be let loose in practice,
might well have been piqued if the honours had been un-
pinned from them and fastened on a middle-aged civilian
lady of the upper middle-classes. There were the Allied
Nations to consider, too. And though my mother would
have been quite prepared to become a second Helen of
Troy, getting along with it in her spare time when she
wasn't busy with her rock garden, her wardrobe, her house-
keeping, and her water colours, it was thought best to leave
things as they were.

It always seems to me a convincing testimony to my
mother's part in the last war that the legend that the last
war was won by somebody's mother is so widespread. I have
met any amount of families with the same belief. They
believe it about their mothers, not mine. But legend is like
that. A truth is spread around, then it gets corrupted. And
the great truth that my mother won the last war passed in
this manner into the larger rumour that the last war was
won by somebody's mother. The fact that people get the
mother wrong does not invalidate the archetypal truth.

My mother won the last war in November, 1914. There
was a British Red Cross depot in our town, where ladies met

*The author is of course referring to the Great War of 1914–1918.

125

to scrape lint, roll bandages, pick over moss for stomach-wound dressings, and make shirts and pyjamas. The lady in charge was a Mrs. Moss-Henry, and when my mother offered her services, Mrs. Moss-Henry set her to cutting out pyjama trousers.

There was a pattern, supplied by the Red Cross authorities, and though it wasn't as good as my mother could have made it, still, it wasn't too bad, and my mother followed it. Maybe she introduced a few improvements, but she didn't win the war on these, so I won't waste time over them.

The next time she went, my mother was surprised when the pyjama trousers she had cut out and handed over to the seamstresses were returned to her. She inquired the reason for this from a fellow-worker who was cutting out pyjama jackets.

'Mrs. Moss-Henry asked me to ask you if you would mind marking where the button and buttonhole are to be.'

'Button?' exclaimed my mother. 'Buttonhole? Ridiculous! The woman's a fool!'

My mother has a decisive mind, a mind that goes straight to essentials. She realized at once that, as the pyjama trousers were made to be fastened by a cord passing through a slot, the addition of a button and buttonhole halfway down the opening was redundant. The other cutter, one of those dull, faithful souls who can only do as they are told, repeated, 'That's what Mrs. Moss-Henry said.'

My mother brooded for a while, but not for long. Five minutes or so. Then, gathering up the pyjama trousers, she rushed from the room in search of Mrs. Moss-Henry.

'I'm not going to mark these trousers for buttons,' she declared. 'It's totally unnecessary.'

Mrs. Moss-Henry, in a very autocratic manner, said that she would be glad if my mother marked the trousers for buttons. It would enable the seamstresses, she said, to know where to sew them on.

My mother explained, clearly, why buttons were redundant. There were no buttons on the pattern which she had been supplied by the Red Cross, she said.

Mrs. Moss-Henry said that it was a paper pattern, unsuited for supporting buttons under hard usage. But buttons had been specified, and must be affixed.

My mother again and categorically registered her protest, and was going on with some good reasons when Mrs. Moss-Henry pretended to hear the telephone bell, and left the room. My mother remained a while with the moss-pickers, amplifying her position. Was it not an outrage, she asked, that our fighting men, who had gone so cheerfully and gallantly to the defence of their country, should, when they came all glorious with wounds into the Red Cross hospitals, be insulted by being buttoned into their pyjama trousers like little boys? Had they not suffered enough for their country and their dear ones left behind? Must they, weak and in pain, be teased with buttoning and unbuttoning themselves? Many of them, she added, would be too weak to do up buttons, anyway.

Some of the moss-pickers agreed with my mother, some sided with Mrs. Moss-Henry. But none were indifferent; they realized that this was a crucial matter. My mother pursued Mrs. Moss-Henry into the bandage-room, and again attacked her.

This time Mrs. Moss-Henry was positively rude to my mother. She said, with a falsely sweet air, that perhaps my mother, as a civilian, was accustomed to civilian pyjamas. Mrs. Moss-Henry's husband had been an Army man, and this enabled Mrs. Moss-Henry to assure my mother that buttons were in order.

The blood of her uncle, who was a brigadier general in the Sudan, boiled in my mother's veins. It was one of those moments when deeds speak louder than words and tearing the pyjama trousers from Mrs. Moss-Henry's grasp she flapped them to and fro in her face.

Mrs. Moss-Henry again retreated. My mother stayed a while with the bandage-rollers, pointing out that even though Mrs. Moss-Henry had passed so much of her life on a baggage wagon, that did not warrant her trying to boss

everything and everybody. Some more arguments then occurred to her, and she went off after Mrs. Moss-Henry.

This running battle continued through the morning.
Finally Mrs. Moss-Henry locked herself in the lavatory. My
mother, careless of the ridicule to which the position exposed her, stood outside the lavatory haranguing Mrs.
Moss-Henry through the door, and the other Red Cross
ladies stood around, some silently supporting my mother,
some silently supporting Mrs. Moss-Henry. At last the combatants dispersed for lunch.

On the morrow my mother, after a sleepless night, returned to the struggle. She found a new force to contend
with. Mrs. Moss-Henry, while refusing to give battle, had
set up a peculiarly insidious propaganda, designed to be-
little my mother's achievements, tarnish her laurels, and
undermine any future advance. This propaganda took the
form of suggesting that it was not really all that important
whether the pyjama trousers had buttons or no; and a
specious plea was made that the output of the workers
would suffer if my mother continued to make such a fuss
about nothing. During the previous morning, it was
alleged, the Red Cross ladies had either done no work at all
or worked less well than usual. Their attention had been
distracted. Mrs. Cory, for instance, had sewn sleeves into
the necks of pyjama jackets instead of into the armholes;
and the garments in question were produced, with striped-
flannel factory chimneys extending where turn-down collars
should have been, as an example of the sort of thing which
might be looked for unless my mother gave up attacking
Mrs. Moss-Henry.

My mother instantly saw through these misrepresen-
tations. Sleeves in the wrong place, she said, were no worse
than buttons where no buttons need be. If output was so important, then time was important, too. Nothing wasted
time more than embroidering needless buttonholes to
corroborate buttons that were perfectly unnecessary. For
her part, she would never grudge time devoted to our splendid soldiers; it was on their behalf, and for their comfort,

that she had joined issue with Mrs. Moss-Henry over the buttons, and she considered it time well spent.

When one of the Moss-Henry minions squirmingly alleged that, after all, the buttons need not incommode the wounded soldiers, for if they found it tiresome to button their pyjama trousers they could leave them unbuttoned, my mother demolished this in an instant. If the buttons were there, regulations to enforce buttoning would be there too. Everyone knew that military-hospital discipline was like that.

Mrs. Moss-Henry entered the room.

'Not still talking about buttons, surely?'

Her tone was sarcastic. My mother replied with firmness, 'I am.'

Mrs. Moss-Henry feigned a yawn.

'I really don't think we want to hear any more about them.'

'You will!' riposted my mother. 'This afternoon I am going to Devonshire House.'

Such words struck awe into every hearer. Devonshire House was the Ark of the Covenant, and the Lion's Jaws. It was the headquarters of the British Red Cross, it was in Piccadilly, and it had been lent to the Red Cross by a duke.

Naturally, my mother put on her best clothes. At the station she was surprised to see Mrs. Moss-Henry, who had put on her best clothes also. Two other ladies—one apiece—completed the deputation. The suburban train took half an hour to get them into London. It was crowded and the four ladies were obliged to travel together, though in silence. Sometimes Mrs. Moss-Henry consulted the papers which she carried in a large portfolio.

My mother had no papers to consult. Instead, she gazed at Mrs. Moss-Henry's hat with an annoying air of unconcern.

The marble hall of Devonshire House was crowded with people waiting for interviews. There was a terrific air of splendour and organization. Secretaries darted to and fro. The two supporters of the deputation began, after a while, to stare about them and whisper, identifying among the waiting throng many stately profiles of England which they had seen in the society papers. Mrs. Moss-Henry behaved as though the aristocracy were nothing to her. So did my mother.

After an hour or so, they were summoned into a large room with desks all round it. Behind each desk was a lady, and each lady was rustling papers. It was as though one stood on some majestic seashore. Their allotted lady gave them a gracious smile, and told them that they were from the Mutton Hill depot. They agreed to this.

As an act of courtesy to the Red Cross organization which had, however misguidedly, placed Mrs. Moss-Henry at the head of the Mutton Hill depot, my mother allowed her to speak first. She spoke next.

The lady behind the desk looked grave; it was obvious that my mother's fearless eloquence had made an impression on her. She said she thought she had better fetch someone else who was more of a specialist. The lady she fetched told them they were from the Mutton Hill depot, and that it was a matter of pyjamas. They answered that it was so.

Mrs. Moss-Henry and my mother restated their positions, exactly, circumstantially, and emphatically. They made it clear (my mother made it clearest) that this was something that must be settled at once, and settled for all time.

The lady who was more of a specialist kept her eyes fixed on the offical trouser pattern, as though a button in invisible ink might be lurking there. At last she said, 'Thank you so much. We quite appreciate your difficulties, and we will write to you shortly.' And she gave them a little dismissing bow.

They were moving away when my mother, with a great surge of indignation and another argument, which had just occurred to her, turned back towards the desk. The lady saw her coming, and held up her hand.

'For the present perhaps you had better leave the buttons off,' she said.

That evening Mrs. Moss-Henry resigned. No letter came from Devonshire House to the Mutton Hill Red Cross depot. After a while my mother resigned, too. There was no need to go on. She had won the war.

In Pimlico

AS I look back on the days of my youth, one of the things that most impresses me about them is the absence of meddling. Except for a nice old lady who said, 'My dear, I hope you won't sleep alone,' I don't recollect anyone showing concern over my future when I left home to set up in London. My father was recently dead, my mother was occupied in being a widow and removing to Devonshire where she would be able to grow gentians. The Carnegie United Kingdom Trust had enlarged its activities from distributing organs to benefiting music in wilder ways. Among these was a project of research into Tudor Church Music. An Editorial Committee had been formed with its headquarters in Westminster, and I from pure inconspicuous merit, or possibly through the unaccountable machinery of fate, had been adjuncted to it, with a salary of three pounds a week and travelling expenses: First Class.

So all that remained was to find myself somewhere to live in London. That was left to me.

Free to enjoy the calm unbridled licence which made everything so much easier in those unmeddlesome days, and with well-defined notions of what I wanted or imperatively did not want, I made expeditions to London, considering neighbourhoods, looking for notice-boards of *To Let* and visiting House Agents, who listened to my simple wants (quiet street, self-containment, enough room for a grand piano, low rental, no church within earshot — for if I was to concentrate on Tudor Church Music I did not want to be distracted by Anglican choir-practices), and gave me orders to view. Some of the places would have suited me ad-

132

mirably, if I had been rich enough to afford them. Others were above fried-fish-shops, dance-halls, or in Ealing. Others just smelled.

At an agents called with simplicity Smith, Smith & Smith, a clerk who seemed to be developing a fatherly feeling towards me, from seeing me so often perhaps, or perhaps from not wanting to see me ever again, suggested that I might be better suited in a hostel. I contained myself and said I thought not. My legs might feel discouraged but my principles were unshaken and life in a hostel was one of the things I imperatively did not want. Resounding with self-respect, I went to a firm called Lomax and Gladstone. Their earlier orders to view proved visionary, but had promise about them. This time I was asked if I would have any objections to Pimlico: there was a flat in Pimlico, just come in that morning, second-floor, self-contained, view of the river, really a unique opportunity, splendid fittings, marble bath, modern geyser . . . I should go at once, for it was bound to be snapped up. I went at once, smirking at this prompt accolade to my principles. Pimlico, too, when one had got to it, had the peculiar appeal of a locality which had begun life with grand ambitions and never achieved them—the sort of place where one would be irresistibly impelled to quotations from Baudelaire.

I was halfway up the stairs when I saw Robert coming down.

'Robert!'

'Sylvia! What on earth are you doing here?'

'I've come to look at a flat.'

'You can't possibly live here.'

'But I think Pimlico's charming.'

'I'm not talking about Pimlico. I'm talking about this house. You cannot possibly take a flat in this house.'

'It's got a marble bath.'

'Marble bath!'

'To lie in a marble bath listening to the tugs hooting on the river. What could be—'

'It *would* have a marble bath.'

'Do they all have marble baths? And how do you know? Robert! Have you just taken my flat? Is that why you were looking so pleased with yourself—and now so taken aback?'

For he had been looking uncommonly pleased with himself—as though he had just come away from a looking-glass. Robert could have hung with credit in any picture gallery: *Portrait of a Young Man, by Sir Joshua Reynolds*; a young man with that slight velvety embonpoint which Sir Joshua conveys so appreciatively; and in Robert's case Sir Joshua, positively licking his lips, had included the mole, black as the black eyes, on his left cheek.

A new light shone on the situation. I exonerated Robert from any designs on my flat. Unless the lady craved for intellectual conversation, she must have found him pleasurable.

Robert was a year younger than me. I felt a tutelary affection for him and hoped in time to make him rather less of an idiot.

'Taken aback? I should jolly well think I was taken aback. And when you talked about taking a flat here—'

'You'd find it embarrassing?'

He shot me a grateful glance. 'I don't see how I could go on coming here.'

I had been reading *The Republic* of Plato. It struck me that the Socratic method might forward my ambition of making Robert rather less of an idiot.

'Do I often embarass you?'

'Well, yes, from time to time. But I get over it.'

'But meeting me here would always embarrass you?'

'Well, what do you expect?'

'Would you be equally embarrassed if I made a point of always using the back stairs?'

'I don't know if there is a back stairs. Besides, there are landings.'

'True. So it is the bodily confrontation with me which you would be embarrassed by?'

'If you must put it that way.'

'If you met four editors of Tudor Church Music coming

134

upstairs, would that be as bad?'

'But why should they come here?'

'To visit me—I shall be in my flat by then—to discuss conjectural readings and *musica ficta* in Taverner's *Salve Intemerata*.'

'That must be screaming fun.'

'What is your idea of fun, Robert?'

'Ordinary fun. Ordinary human fun, nothing clever about it.'

'But if you heard us discussing *musica ficta* in Taverner's *Salve Intemerata*, would you be embarrassed?'

'Yawn my head off, more likely.'

'But you would not be embarrassed?'

'I don't see why I should be.'

'Good. We seem to have got that much settled. And if you came in and found us eating—say—winkles—'

'Winkles? What on earth are you driving at?'

'You'll see.'

For some one inexperienced in the Socratic method, Robert was coming along pretty well. In a few minutes more I'd have brought him to admit that fornication and musicology could go on under the same roof and neither parties feel the worse for it. Socrates would have carried it further, but I thought I'd leave it at that.

'Do you like winkles?' I continued.

'Not particularly. Aren't they supposed to be good for the brain?'

'Then it would seem that there are two approaches to eating winkles: one, to improve the intellect, the other because you like the taste.'

'Might bring off both.'

'And that the approaches are different—you admit as much, for you say "both". Well, suppose you found me and the editors of Tudor Church Music in my flat eating winkles—'

'That's enough about your flat! I tell you, you can't possibly take a flat in this house. It's impossible, it's out of the question, it won't do. If you don't drop the idea—'

'Yes?'

'I'll tell your mother.'

As I looked at him the mole twitched. We broke into wild laughter, and laughed and laughed till an acrid voice from above said 'Hush!' and we stole away. A couple of days later I found a flat in Bayswater. It was draughty and in-commodious, but had ample room for the grand piano.

Being a Lily

WHEN Jesus said, 'Consider the lilies of the field, how they grow; they toil not, neither do they spin: and yet I say unto you that even Solomon in all his glory was not arrayed like one of these,' he was making an economic statement. Solomon's outgoings must have been appalling: wives, concubines, children, priests, eunuchs, functionaries, visitors, ceremonials, pensioners, the stables, the upkeep of his botanical and zoological gardens, the obligation to tip everybody in sight — it is not surprising that he wrote those wistful passages about contentment and the simple life. Subsequent Solomons have invented their evasions. They live very quietly and don't entertain, they buy works of art which will go to the nation in lieu of death duties, they can't afford a family. But they can't escape responsibilities. The state becomes dependent on them; they are taxed for its support; the richer they are the more they are taxed, and if they become less rich it is no real pleasure to them because they dread poverty. Either way, ruin stares them in the face. The lily lives within its means. It knows no obligations, it has no little lilies dependent on it. As it cannot toil or spin, it has no ambition to better its lot by doing so. It doesn't even do the best it can. It just does.

For a few years of my life I approximated to the lily state. I had a salary of £150 a year, which I drew from the bosom of the Carnegie United Kingdom Trust, much as the lilies drew their stipend of chemicals from the soil of Palestine. I had a yearly allowance of £100 from my family, tantamount to a Palestinian rainfall. My flat in Bayswater, London, was

137

rented at £90. I lived with economic trimness on £160 a year. I had no dependents, no claims on that £160 except when my friends needed to borrow from me. From time to time I felt hungry, and in winter I often felt cold. But I never felt poor.

I was fortunate in having few preconceived ideas. Preconceived ideas embody the wisdom of the ages; they are bound to be at least ten years out of date; and as I began my life as a lily in the autumn of 1917 the ideas of 1907 would not have very precisely applied. But a few had adhered to me. One of these was that good managers always keep accounts, superlatively good managers by double entry. After ten days or so of carefree shopping around, discovering a fishmonger who sold winkles, the hit-or-miss rewardingness of broken biscuits, the convenience of ready-made Beef Olives (small wads of hard-pressed mince flavoured by machinery and cased in sanguine glaze, and one soon grew tired of them), I called myself to heel and bought an account book, and coming home with my purchases I sat down to enter them; but on the one page only, as I did not think I would bother about double entry just then:

Winkles	4d
2 bread rolls	2d
$\frac{1}{4}$ lb butter	2s
Watercress	2d
Violets	3d
Carrots	5d
Account Book	9d

I added it up. It came to four shillings and a penny. This was more than I reckoned for. I was alarmed. Yet I did not seem to have been extravagant. The violets were licensed: some eminent person — Goethe, perhaps, or Ruskin or Seneca — had said that to spend nothing on the Beautiful was an ill-balanced economy; and I had spent almost twice as much on the carrots. The truth blazed out on the page. *Account Book 9d*. To spend all that good money on an account book was waste and ostentation. I couldn't call the

138

money back, but at least I would not squander any more
time on keeping accounts.

The discrepancy between the bread rolls and the butter
did not alarm me. Butter was then eight shillings a pound.
As I could do nothing about this, I accepted it, reclining on
Pragmatism. Eggs were a shilling each; and as one of the
few things I knew how to cook was an omelette it was quite a
tussle to recline. But when I came home one wet December
morning and cracked the egg I had carried so carefully and
so hopefully and found it was a bad one, I determined on
action and put the egg in a teacup. Holding the teacup in
one hand, supporting an umbrella with the other, I walked
up Queen's Way, Bayswater, to confront the grocer.
Placing the teacup before him, I said with dignity that I was
not prepared to pay a shilling for a bad egg, and that he
must replace it with a good one. He made some general
remarks on the sad lot of those dealing in eggs and passed to
the larger theme of the hardships of war. I repeated my
demand for a replacement. Scrambling unwillingly out of
the trenches, the grocer said it hardly seemed fair. There
were other customers in the shop, and I felt they were inclined to side with the grocer, self-interest overriding
abstract notions of justice. Then a burly voice with an Irish
accent remarked, 'The lady's right. It's the Law of the Land.'
No Lord Chief Justice in his ermine could have looked more
monumentally irreproachable, though in point of fact he
ran errands for the betting shop round the corner. We
unanimously accepted his word for it. The grocer gave me
another egg. It was a good one.

I feel no remorse about that egg, and I don't think the
grocer held it against me — much. Good manners obliged
me to go on patronizing him, and, though we never
achieved cordiality, we were able to converse with decency
about the non-animate, such as biscuits. What my conscience still brings to mind when I have exhausted all other
subjects for repentance is the Hoover salesman. Yet it wasn't
altogether my fault. Twice he had knocked at my door and
assured me that ladies who bought vacuum cleaners led

changed lives and never regretted it, and that a demonstration would involve me in nothing; all he asked was that I should see for myself. And twice over I had told him in all seriousness that I could not afford to buy a Hoover, that I couldn't undertake to pay by instalments, that he must go away and forget me. Apparently, something about me was unforgettable—some housewifely smut on my nose, perhaps, or perhaps the vista of grime and neglect he glimpsed through the doorway. For he came again; and this time my mind must have been elsewhere, for before I could stop him he had come into my sitting-room and writhed a great serpent after him. 'It's no use,' I said. 'I can't afford it. I don't want it.' But he replied that if he could have the loan of a stepladder he would begin with the curtains.

I fetched the stepladder. He and the serpent ascended it. I think that briefly I had in my heart a mute desperate prayer that he might fall off and end it that way. But the prayer was brief. Why should I wish him to end untimely something which he had set his heart on? Such a fine opportunity, too, to show what his Hoover could do if really put to it. When he had done with the curtains, I would unflinchingly send the poor man away. But by the time he was down the ladder and working on the rugs I was furtively strewing cigarette butts in the serpent's way for the satisfaction of watching them being swallowed up and machinery triumphing over matter. I must say, the result of all this was marvellous. I would not have known my sitting-room for my own, and I was able to say with real feeling in my voice how sorry I was I could not afford a Hoover when I gave him five shillings I could not afford either. But it was a shabby proceeding, and if there were a Society for the Promotion of Kindness to Hoover Salesmen (S.P.K.H.S.) I would subscribe conscience money to it.

In other respects, my virtues walked their narrow round, and I don't think I did anything reprehensible unless it were putting on my hat whenever my doorbell rang so that in case of bores I could mendaciously exclaim, 'Oh, how unfortunate! I am just going out,' and walk as far as the

Underground with them — a mere hundred yards and well worth it.

There was no incentive to do anything reprehensible. I was happy and contented as I was. If I wanted diversion, I had London to divert myself in. If I wanted a breath of the Orient, I could snuff it in Penny Fields or watch a local Archimandrite buying cod fillet (Bayswater abounded in Archimandrites) and wonder why the religious life leads inevitably to cod. If I wished to feel ennobled, I had the Wren Orangery at hand. If I needed amusement, London is rich in public statuary, and if the weather wasn't suitable for that, I could sit indoors reading *Tom Jones*. And any impulses towards lawbreaking were looked after by thrift. For though thrift in moderation cannot be called anti-social, I don't know anything to equal it for giving one a sense of roguery and cardsharping. Every little advantage I filched from circumstances, every penny I stretched into three halfpence, every profitable abstention, every exercise of forethought, every stratagem and purloined opportunity made me feel as gay as Macheath. I used to walk into the British Museum, expand in that warmth, smell that ambrosial floor polish, and settle down to my Carnegie United Kingdom Trust affair in the Manuscript Room, smirking at the thought that for hours and hours I would be kept warm by public expenditure, and more than half believing that this was due to my own unaided cleverness and good management. But it must be thrift in moderation. I was careful to eschew carnal mortifications; I never debased myself by giving up smoking.

On fuller consideration of the lilies, however, I suspected I wasn't being all I should be: I was deficient in the article of being arrayed. I don't mean my outward raiment. Like the ladies of Boston, I had my hat. But I lacked, so to speak, sheen, moral splendour, the gloriousness and baroque of extravagance. I was happy and contented and doing, I considered, nicely; but doing nicely was not enough. I should occasionally blaze, and blaze on my own initiative, not always leave it to Sir Christopher Wren.

141

One cannot blaze to order. I remember standing outside a shop window which displayed a great number of objects, some shiny, some furry, all in their various ways coquettish, or rendered so, if inherently sober like alarm clocks, by bows. A placard in the centre of the window read 'AC-CEPTABLE GIFTS,' and I thought morosely that if taken in the leanest sense of the words this was an adequate statement. I felt very differently going out of my way to linger outside the window of a gallery where the sole object was a little Courbet of two dark-green pears. I blazed, all right. But the little Courbet was beyond the bounds of any extravagance I could reach to. A few weeks later, it was gone. So were the Acceptable Gifts, and replaced by bed linen, for it was the season of White Sales. I had noticed this and walked on when I realized that something was about to take place in me; not, as I first surmised, a sneeze: an ex-travagance. I was going to buy that pair of sheets. Ap-prehending without conscious vision, I had seen that depth of white, that smooth swan web of fine linen—which is as tough, too, as the noble swan. I knew I would have them. I knew I would have to fight for them. For Prudence was yelling in my ears about the electricity bill, and half of my mind was ranged on her side, reminding me that thrift was not only for fun—that freedom depended on it, since if I couldn't live within my £160 I should have to leave my stately solitude and doss down in some dreary receptacle for working girls. I turned round and walked back to the shop, and Prudence followed me, now yammering about justification. And on the threshold of the shop the answer glided into my mind, smooth as linen. The sheets would do to shroud me in. So I went in and bought them.

Battles Long Ago

WHEN I read some while ago of the rumpus in the Belgian Parliament about whether or no King Baudouin should attend the funeral of His Late Majesty King George VI, my mind swept me back to the autumn of 1914, when my life was convulsed by King Baudouin's grandfather, and by the van de Berghes and the van Dalens. Disregarding treaties of neutrality, the German Army had marched into Belgium, and King Baudouin's grandfather had called up his small army to resist them. The invasion was conducted in accordance with the best Prussian traditions — that is to say, with a savage mistrust of anything not in a military uniform, and a great number of terrorized people got out of Belgium as fast as they could and came to England.

I was twenty then, and living in a town on the northern outskirts of London, and I had already attached myself, in a sort of girl-of-all-work capacity, to a local organization that had coagulated from a flurry of centripetal helpfulness and was called the War Help. One afternoon, I found myself in the back seat of a car, behind Mr. Bale, who was the head of the organization, and his chauffeur, being whirled at twenty-five miles an hour towards the Alexandra Palace, a sombre Victorian construction intended to supply North London with something like the Crystal Palace. Though smaller and less crystalline, it was equally high-minded. Dog shows were held there, and concerts, and now it contained Belgian refugees.

I was twenty, and a European, and I had never seen a refugee. This now seems remarkable, but Mr. Bale was

143

twice my age and I don't think he had ever seen a refugee, either. There had been an appeal to householders to take refugees into their homes, and Mr. Bale for the War Help was going to the Alexandra Palace to see about it. He vanished into some administrative sanctum, leaving me in a long gallery roofed with glass (a winter garden, perhaps; I remember there were palms) and full of people sitting on benches. A continuous morose din resounded from the glass roof. Yet no one appeared to be talking. The refugees sat shoulder to shoulder, as dumped and mute as their bundles. Their faces expressed nothing but fatigue and stupefaction. From among this parterre of homeless people, all shapeless and anonymous through misery and lack of sleep, my eye picked out a woman who was holding a bundled child and a coffeepot.

Throughout the return journey, I sat thinking about her. When the car stopped, I had everything clear in my mind. It was no use hoping to plant out Belgian refugees by ones and twos in kind English homes where tea is drunk instead of coffee. It would never work. The proper solution was to have houses where several families could live together in a Belgian way. I explained my theory to Mr. Bale, and added that as far as our town went, I would manage it. Mr. Bale was a remarkable man in many ways; for example, he was the only man in our town who had a Japanese gardener with the Rising Sun of Japan embroidered on the seat of his trousers. Now he said I could get on with it, and report to him at the end of three days.

Standing empty in the middle of the town was a house that belonged to the local builder. He agreed to lend it to me and threw in the additional loan of a handcart. People I knew, and presently people I didn't know, lent me furniture, crockery, cutlery, bedding, cooking pots. Tradespeople gave me a week's supply of ordinary household staples, the coal merchant put in half a ton of coal, the water board and the electric-light company turned on water and lighting, and on the third day I made my calm report to Mr. Bale, who notified the proper authorities that ten of the refugees at Alexandra Palace could be accommodated in our town.

Meanwhile, a pair of Belgian refugees had already been domiciled in a local household, and I went to call on them, hoping to pick up some guidance. They were a mother and a son, and not at all the Alexandra Palace kind of refugee. The mother smelled of scent more strongly and deliciously than ladies in our town ever smelled on an ordinary weekday, and had brought a sable coat—if you have one, a more sensible thing to bring than a coffeepot. The son kissed my hand—a new experience. The mother did most of the talking. In a voice brimming with sympathy, she spoke of the disappointment I was bringing on myself. So young, she said, and belonging to such a quiet, well-behaved nation, I could have no idea what I would run into if I devoted myself to the sort of refugees I had seen at the Palace—the sweepings, she said, of the Antwerp slums. They would steal and riot; they would be dirty; they would bite the hand that fed them. Furthermore, the English did not realize that there were two kinds of Belgians.

I said that I had already been warned about Flemish separatism.

That was mere politics, she said. The real dividing line, the gulf, was between those who practised their religion and those who had none. I would find that the Palace refugees had no religion—not a shred of it. Her son confirmed this, and added that I must be prepared for them to say '*non-ante*' for '*quatre-vingt-dix*' if they spoke any French at all.

The greater proportion of the refugees at the Palace were Flemish-speaking, and this strengthened my conviction that it would be easier for our refugees to move into their house without any assistance from me. It was not till some hours after their arrival that I went round to introduce myself. A very old man was standing in the doorway, wearing a blue jersey and looking silvery with virtue. Meeting my eye, he bowed and remarked, '*Mauvais temps.*' It was a perfectly fine afternoon. I had read many little plays by Maurice Maeterlinck in which just such old men, wandering in and

145

out of woods, conveyed an ineffable lot by short sentences only obliquely applicable. Though I had reverenced these dramas, I had not thought of them as true to contemporary Belgian life. Now I seemed to be in the middle of one.

Inside the house, there wasn't a breath of M. Maeterlinck. A short, stout man with pale-blue eyes and a Vercingetorix moustache was putting up a shelf, all the furniture had been rearranged, and some women were holding an indignation meeting in the kitchen because there was no soap jelly. The indignation was plain enough, but I should not have known the cause of it if a young man, hovering on the outskirts of their fury, had not told me, in French. I asked him to interpret my regrets, and no doubt he did so, but quite unavailingly, for the women went on raging and picking up bars of yellow soap only to throw them down with gestures of abhorrence. I asked him how one said in Flemish 'I am sorry.' He told me and it sounded like Greek, but, hoping for the best, I reverberated it.

The effect was electrical. A fine old Bellona by Rubens hugged the breath out of me, and what parts of me emerged from her embrace were patted or warmly smacked by the lesser furies. They let go eventually, and waited to hear what else I could say. I mutely held out a large basket of damsons that I had brought along with me, and five minutes later we were all making jam together and singing the 'Brabançonne' in a kitchen that was already permeated with Flemish cookery and smelled of vinegar, like an ant heap.

Reeling home, I said over to myself that the four pairs of very pale-blue eyes were van de Berghe; that the family group of van Dalens included Bellona and Mauvais Temps, who were surnamed Geraerds and were Mrs. van Dalen's parents; that the young man who had told me how to say 'I am sorry' in Flemish was Jules and the swarthy young woman called Léopoldine was his sister, and they were not related to either the van de Berghes or the van Dalens.

Relying on what the woman with the sable coat had told me, I assumed that all these nice, friendly people were

146

among the godless. So when a lady in the town brought me
a rosary she had picked up in the street and which she felt
sure must have been dropped by one of my Belgians, though
I said I would make inquiries, I inwardly pooh-poohed the
thought. The rosary was a very grand one, so elegant and
mother-of-pearled that something told me it might be better not to exhibit it. Instead, I would just mention it the
next time I went to the house.

The French for 'rosary' is '*un chapelet*,' and when I next
found van Dalens and van de Berghes in conclave, and
wanted the word, I couldn't recollect it. This thing that had
been picked up, I explained, was an object connected with
religion, an aid to piety, used in personal devotions or on
Sundays. At this point in my explanation, Mr. van de
Berghe's countenance (with the Vercingetorix moustache)
lit up with intellectual dayspring and he explaimed, '*Le
dimanche? Ah, oui! Les bretelles.*'

Identifying braces as a means to devotion, putting up
shelves and polishing floors, going about garlanded in Annette and Agnès, his two little girls, Mr. van de Berghe was
dear to me as my own right hand, and I generally turned to
him as my interpreter, for though he hadn't much French,
he had a heart-and-soul interest in everything that was
going on. I daresay I should have left it at braces if
Léopoldine had not come in a moment later. (She and Jules
were apt to keep by themselves, being socially timid — and
slightly superior in class, as the young usually are.)
Léopoldine, like Jules, was bilingual. She supplied the right
word and interpreted my inquiry to the van Dalens. Far
from being godless, the van Dalens knew all about rosaries,
though nothing about this one, and revealed themselves as
practising Catholics. Horrified at my remissness, I told
them where to find the Catholic church, and said that I
would ask Father Macarthy to look out for them. I noticed
that Mr. and Mrs. van Dalen instantly began to look more
respectable. (They looked respectable anyhow, but the in-
crement was unmistakable.) I hoped they would come to
look happier, but it was Mrs. Geraerds who seemed

positively pleased. As I was going away, she beckoned me into a bedroom and showed me her bad leg. Just as I had never seen refugees, I had never seen a bad leg. After that, she took my education in hand and taught me a number of useful Flemish substantives, so that on my brighter days I could follow her round the house, rattling off such nouns as 'bolster,' 'potatoes,' and 'pepper pot.'

I was intending to learn some verbs, too, but I never found time for that, partly because I had been lent a second empty house and was busy fitting it up, and partly because I had become encrusted with a committee. The members of this committee were all hardened in good works and passionately addicted to post-mortems. It wasn't long before they told me they had learned, through someone who wished to remain anonymous, that the relationship between Jules and Léopoldine was not that of brother and sister. The committee also told me that the guilty pair must be re-turned to the Alexandra Palace. I wasn't so badly encrusted that I couldn't dish a majority decision by blackmail. Both houses, I reminded them, had been lent to *me*, and both lenders would withdraw their loans if I asked them to. When that was done, I said I would watch with interest how the committee got on with the sequel.

Jules and Léopoldine were not returned to the Alexandra Palace, but they had to be torn apart and were kept captive in separate lodging houses until their wedding could be arranged. Fortunately, they seemed to have no objection to this interpolation to their private lives and told me very amiably that they had always meant to get married at some time or other. Léopoldine said that it was the van Dalens who had been the talebearers. The van Dalen group were solidly Flemish-speakers, the greeting from Maeterlinck being all the French Mr. Geraerds possessed, and used by him merely as a form of how-d'you-doing. I did not see how a van Dalen could have poured a Flemish tale into an English ear, until one day the woman with the sable coat came across the street to condole with me on the disillusioning experience. She had told me at our first

148

meeting that she understood no more than two words of Flemish, but no doubt she was bilingual enough to understand a church-porch confidence.

The inmates of the second house were picked at the Alexandra Palace by a committee member versed in sexual morality. Unfortunately, she disregarded, or was unaware of, the danger of mixing Flemings with French-speaking Belgians. The night after their arrival, our simple townsfolk stood in awed rows outside the house listening to the shindy going on inside, while jugs, plates, saucepans, and finally the policeman were hurled into the street. By morning, the house was a shambles and the nice question of Flemish separatism as far from a solution as ever.

That was a Saturday. The next morning, soon after breakfast, Annette van de Berghe arrived breathless at my house to say would I please come at once to—as far as I could gather—get her father out of the bath? I went at once. Mauvais Temps was standing outside, as usual, in company with the quiet married couple who had replaced Jules and Léopoldine, but from the second floor came a roar of impetuous conversation, accompanied by hammerings and the noise of running water. The rest of the household, except for Mr. van de Berghe, was in a cluster outside the bathroom. I supposed him to be having a fit inside, and that they were all concerned to rescue him, though I could not reconcile that with Mrs. van Dalen's being in her best and blackest outdoor clothes, while Mr. van Dalen was in his shirtsleeves and brandishing a straight-edged razor. Seeing my alarmed glance at the razor, Annette said reassuringly, 'Pour la Messe.' And then it burst on me that Mr. van de Berghe was obstructing the churchgoing van Dalens and that what I had on my hands was religious war.

There was a sink in the kitchen, and I did not feel that there would be any essential impiety if Mr. van Dalen shaved there instead of in the bathroom. I tried to express this by gestures and some of the valuable substantives I had learned from Mrs. Geraerds. How little I understood

149

religious war! Mr. van Dalen would shave nowhere but in the bathroom. Mr. van de Berghe was in the bathroom and would not come out. He did turn the water off, however, and by making a great noise myself I managed to still the tumult and asked Mr. van de Berghe, through the door, to come out of the bathroom. He replied that he would come out when he had finished washing. The van Dalens and Mrs. Geraerds then began telling him how long he had been there already, and the taps were again turned on. Once more I roared down the van Dalens and called on Mr. van de Berghe, this time appealing to his better nature. Once more the taps were turned off, and Mr. van de Berghe made me a formal apology, as on behalf of the Belgian nation, for the ungrateful conduct of the van Dalens. Wasn't it enough that I should work so hard during the week, without disturbing me on a Sunday? He then spoke in Flemish, and presumably gave a translation of these sentiments, for the van Dalens burst into an uproar of acrimony. So far, Mrs. van de Berghe had taken no part in the altercation except to giggle and utter occasional exclamations. But now she joined in and said something so outrageously cogent that Mrs. van Dalen slapped her face with a prayer book. Mrs. van de Berghe tore off Mrs. van Dalen's churchgoing hat, Mrs. Geraerds rushed to her daughter's defence, and Annette and Agnès, fierce as ferrets, whisked round the outskirts of the fray.

I thought of Mrs. Geraerds' bad leg, and of Mr. van Dalen's razor. Mr. van Dalen, scorning to fight with women, now gave his whole attention to hammering on the bathroom door, seeming almost as anxious to get out of reach of the combatants as to get in and shave. I hoped that Mr. van de Berghe's feelings as a family man might bring him out, if only to protect his ferrets. Instead, he expressed himself by a new method with the taps, turning them on and off, on and off, as if they were an instrument of percussion. To the accompaniment of this maddening rhythm, Mrs. van Dalen, Mrs. van de Berghe, Mrs. Geraerds, and the ferrets fought themselves to a standstill.

150

Those who have not heard a quarrel in Flemish can have no notion what a relief it is to the ear when it leaves off. Even with Mr. van Dalen still hammering, and Mr. van de Berghe still playing on his taps, and the low, bruised murmur coming from the people gathered outside, the effect of silence was solemn indeed. I felt a vandal to break it. But once again I addressed Mr. van de Berghe through the door, this time sternly, telling him that if he did not come out immediately, I would break the door open.

Too chivalrous to comment on the discrepancy between my threat and my ability to enforce it, he answered that he would be out as soon as he had put his clothes on, and added that he felt sure that Miss would not desire him to appear without them. I looked at my watch. Even if Mr. van de Berghe were not feeling this proper regard for my modesty, there was not now time enough for Mr. van Dalen to shave before starting for Mass. Smoothing Annette's embattled flaxen plaits, I told her that her father would be out almost immediately and that there was no further need for anyone to get upset. Then, like a ministering angel whose task is done, I glided away.

Unfortunately, my task was not done, and well I knew it. All I could do was to become impartially aloof and wait for the next Sunday. The lockout was repeated a week later, and this time Mr. van de Berghe, taking no chances, occupied the bathroom from before daylight. On the following Saturday evening, the van Dalens went to steal the key. They found that the door was locked. True, Mr. van de Berghe was in the kitchen, blamelessly occupied with some beetroot, but, for all that, the door had been locked from the outside, the key was missing, and it was too late to get a locksmith.

Then came Léopoldine's wedding and, like a Jubilee, put everything right. Mr. van de Berghe and Mr. van Dalen, shaven to perfection, attended the ceremony — a religious one, performed by Father Macarthy. Rice was thrown, and afterwards we breakfasted on sausages, fritters, vinegar, and a wonderful cake offered by the baker to the first

151

Belgian wedding in our town. Jules and Léopoldine settled into a flat. The second house, refurnished and wholly loyal to the Lion of Flanders, turned its ground floor into a workshop, where wooden toys were made, and sold at a shameless profit for the Belgian Red Cross. The van Dalens went unimpeded about their religious duties. Solidarity was restored. So much so, indeed, that when the committee developed doubts about Mauvais Temps, who was alleged to be a secret milk drinker, sipping from the bottles left on neighbouring doorsteps, Mr. van de Berghe stood forth as an unshakeable witness to his silvery integrity.

Troublemaker

NOT long ago the British Broadcasting Corporation opened a recital of chamber music with the slow movement of the Emperor string quartet by Haydn, whose theme most people recognize as 'Deutschland Über Alles'. This happened to come immediately after a news broadcast. A number of listeners who didn't listen long enough to discover that the theme was followed by variations concluded that the B.B.C. reactionaries had placed this tune with bad intentions, and hurried to write letters of protest to newspapers, members of Parliament, and the B.B.C. By the time that other people, better informed, had written further letters to say how silly the first people were, there was quite a nice little uproar. This did not surprise me. Already I had known that tune for a troublemaker.

When I was a child, I lived at Borogove, the seat of a famous English public school renowned, as are all famous English public schools, for its irrational customs and the piety with which they are defended. My father was a master there, so on Sundays I was taken to worship in the Hencoop—a transept of the school chapel set apart for the wives and daughters of the staff. The opposite transept was set apart for Old Borogovians.

At Borogove, the singing is conducted in sturdy congregational unison, and the choir is drawn from distinguished athletes, whose achievements command respect and following from the rest of the congregation. It is therefore grand to be in the choir. The first and last Sundays of the term are marked by one or the other of a pair of hymns, one beginning, 'Lord, behold us with Thy blessing,' and containing aspirations for improvement, the other beginning, 'Lord, dismiss us with Thy blessing,' and expressing hope that shortcomings may be overlooked. These hymns are in use at most educational establishments, but at Borogove they had peculiar traditionalism and patina because the six-line stanzas were sung to the tune of 'Deutschland Über Alles,' which is an eight-line tune.

It is obvious that there are two expedients by which this discrepancy may be overcome. One is to repeat two lines of the stanza, the other to cut out two lines of the tune. Borogove adopted the second expedient. It elided the third and fourth lines and the effect was arresting, not unlike what one feels when one thinks there is going to be another step down on the stairs and there isn't: a jolt, a temporary dizziness and disbelief, followed by the acceptance of a hard fact. But it was a custom and nobody dreamed of questioning it (nobody at Borogove) till, in the year 1915, there was a movement to taboo German music as being full of corrupting implications, of enemy origin, and not as good as Allied products anyway. When this movement reached Borogove, the school music master began in a serpentine way to inflame public opinion against such things as the Venusberg music, and especially to deplore the use of what was really the German national anthem for our two dearest and most valued hymns.

This, of course, was very reprehensible of him — he should not have taken up such a shoddy crusade — and it was also injudicious, for his knowledge of the world and of Borogove should have warned him not to raise spirits he might not be able to appease. Largely through his efforts, the German national anthem was cast away and he was requested to compose a substitute.

He did so, and it was considered to be very melodious and national. It was taught to the athletic choir, and when they were pretty sure of it, there were weekday practises for the whole congregation, so that even if the choir should have a temporary aberration, the rest of us should not be left like sheep without a shepherd. Some of the masters taught it to their wives. No pains were spared.

Meanwhile, other masters, who also happened to be Old Borogovians, were oppressed with doubts and disaffections and a sharp sense that an impiety had been committed. The new tune might be all very well — patriotic, no doubt — but it was new. That in itself was bad. But it was not even like the old one, and that was worse. It was new, it was different. It lacked the trenchancy of an eight-line tune with the third and fourth lines left out; no mere six-line performance could achieve quite the same vitalizing effect. Torn between two loyalties, they chose the local one: though the perpetuation of the German national anthem in the school chapel might make a bad impression on the God of Battles, they decided to take a chance on it and to preserve Borogove whatever else might go.

On the last Sunday evening of the term, we saw the Old Borogovian transept filling up with more and more Old Borogovians — Old Borogovians of all sorts and sizes and ages, but all wearing a stern and devoted demeanour. The sermon ended, the last hymn was given out, and the lights dimmed, but they always did that, for the lighting and the organ were run off the same engine. The congregation rose, the organ emitted the usual low preliminary 'pom,' and, led by the choir, we broke into the new tune with confidence and *brio*. But after a couple of loud lines we became aware of a deep, mooing discordancy, which proceeded from the Old Borogovian transept and presently declared itself as the Old Borogovians singing the old tune. Otherwise well organized, the dissentient faction had not thought of rehearsals. Consequently, it took them a little time to get together. But after a ragged start they showed their real quality, and by the end of the first verse ('May thy children, may thy children, Ne'er again thy spirit grieve') they were roaring as one.

Presumably there were a few rallying words in the organ loft. Anyhow, the second verse began with the athletic

155

choir showing a lot of fight and most of the congregation supporting them with great loyalty; only about twenty-five per cent or so wandered off to the Old Borogovians because they knew the old tune so much better, and many of these returned to the right path when summoned by the trumpet stop. The new tune had all the advantages of the athletic choir, seventy-five per cent of the congregation, and the reinforcements of the organ console, but Haydn fought along with the Old Borogovians and, even though mutilated, was a powerful ally. The second verse was a draw.

There were still two more verses, and the Old Borogovians, who were, as they were wont to describe themselves on Founder's Day, 'shorter in wind though in memory long,' realized that they couldn't maintain their full force to the end, so in the third round they went in to kill. They soon had the advantage, and they scored a decisive punch by holding on to their last note (I really can't say whether by accident or design) after their rivals had left off, and then intensifying it into a screech of defiance that rang through the sacred edifice. The issue was no longer in doubt.

In the last verse, the Old Borogovians — except for a sprinkling of athletes, one or two Boadiceas in the Hencoop, and the organ, which had gone off into a sort of free fugue — had it all their own way. The rest of us just stood there while the victorious defenders of the old faith gathered themselves together for a parting plea to the Almighty that those returning, those returning, might be made more faithful than before.

It is part of the Borogove tradition not to have an amen after hymns, so when the last Old Borogovian voice had died away, there was no comment until the school chaplain ejaculated, 'Let us pray.' The plea for more faithfulness, however, was granted. Next term the Lord beheld us with his blessing to the tune of 'Deutschland Über Alles,' omitting the third and fourth lines.

156

Deep in the Forest

I HAD persuaded my nephew, Oliver, to join me in taking some German-conversation lessons from Fräulein Hildegarde, the Prewitts' new household companion. I could not put out of my mind that heavy, stupid, melancholy voice saying, 'If I earned a little extra money by giving lessons, then would I buy English books to improve myself—and chocolate to eat by night.' She had lost pounds since coming to the Prewitts.

'Think of the Prewitts' meals, Oliver!' I had said. 'I can't stand by and watch even a hired *Hitlerjugend* starve. And we can learn useful German, for once. Like "rear axle", and "filling station", and "hot-water bag". Whatever one feels about the Nazis, it's imbecile to leave them the monopoly of knowing the German for "rear axle."'

So at our first lesson I explained firmly to Hildegarde that there need be no German grammar. Both Oliver and I, I said, had learned German grammar in our respective childhoods, and it would, no doubt, come back to us in the course of conversation. What we needed, I continued, was a more contemporary vocabulary. Perhaps Hildegarde might begin by talking to us, slowly, about automobiles.

She thought this over.

'Deep in the forest,' she began.

Hildegarde spoke so slowly, and her diction was so exceedingly simple, that even to us it was quite clearly apparent that there was once an aged forester who had two fair-haired children, children so imbued with family affection that they always addressed each other as Brotherling and Sisterling. Presently a wicked stepmother was added to

157

the list of characters, the forester turned into a Birdling, and Brotherling and Sisterling left the unbalanced home and went out to seek their fortunes, still keeping to the forest. After quite a series of conversations with various animals, conversations cut short by Birdling's remarking from a tree, 'Speak not to that bad animal. It means you no good,' Sisterling was married to a prince, Brotherling to a princess, Birdling was restored to human form, and the stepmother was boiled. At the close of the narrative, Hildegarde said, 'It is an old German fairy tale.'

I remarked that it was nice and easy to follow. Hildegarde replied, 'We have many such.'

Time proved how true this was. Do what we would—persuade, hint, rebel—Hildegarde, with an inflexible flow of pure and simple German, bore us into that forest. Sometimes the stories might begin 'High on yonder hill' or 'Deep beneath the still blue lake,' but after a paragraph or two, the forest was once more rustling overhead and stretching for miles on every side. Sometimes we got into it by hunting the deer, sometimes by following one of those garrulous Birdlings. Once we got there looking for a rose, and quite often we just got there by losing our way.

'It's because we're so mute,' I said to Oliver.

'Spellbound,' said he.

'If we could get in first, firmly, with questions, if we asserted ourselves—'

'We should just be carried kicking and yelling into her forest. It's less trouble to go quietly. I tell you, she doesn't know how to talk about anything else.'

'Everyone can talk about themselves,' I said. And privately I looked up the German words with which to ask some plain, straightforward questions—the sort of questions which are usually considered personal and ill-bred.

It worked better than I had dared hope. At our next lesson, we discovered that Hildegarde was nineteen and had been vaccinated in the leg, that her father was the

158

mayor of a provincial town, and that his favourite sport was fishing. Streams, we knew by experience, led into the forest. Oliver inquired hastily whether the town had many factories.

'It is a beautiful town. All round it there are trees. In the spring they blossom —'

I remembered another question and put it quickly. 'What do you do on holidays?'

'We go for bicycle rides. It is delightful. We go into the forest —'

Oliver left the room with a bang.

'Well,' he inquired, when we met again, 'What had Birdling got to say this time?'

'Not a word. We just stayed in the forest long enough to eat cakes and drink coffee. Then we bicycled out again.'

'Do you mean to say that you actually talked? Talked like reasoning beings?'

I nodded.

'What did you talk about?'

'General topics.'

I smiled at Oliver as aunts are wont to smile, and much to my relief he resented it as a nephew should, and asked no more questions. For I should have found it painful to divulge that, the moment his back was turned, Hildegarde had announced that now, being alone together, we could talk of such things as we, being women, were interested in. The subjects which we might be interested in revealed themselves as gossip about common acquaintances — that is to say, about the Prewitts; cakes and sandwiches; and the place of woman in the universe. The place of woman in the universe was, according to Hildegarde, steadfastly simple. She had first to bring forth warriors, and then be a comfort to them. In Hildegarde's case it developed, the order of these obligations had been inverted. She showed me a quantity of snapshots of the various warriors she had been a comfort to already, getting her hand in, I supposed, before proceeding to the remainder of her mission.

159

The comforted ones were of all shapes and sizes and ages, but all had much the same expression, or, rather, lack of expression. They all had their eyes very wide open and their jaws very tight shut, and the general effect was as though they were stifling themselves for a matter of principle. It was such a relief to come on a middle-aged warrior thoughtfully scratching his back and wearing a tight striped bathing suit that I cried out, 'Who's this one?'

'That one? Oh, that's my father.'

And she flipped him over hastily. Not dignified enough, I supposed. At nineteen, one is sensitive about one's father, even if he is a mayor.

Partly from curiosity, partly, I must admit, from malice—for in or out of her forest, Hildegarde was really *too* densely self-righteous—I set myself to pry out some more about her father. Each inquiry produced the same result: the same look, stubborn and slightly alarmed, the same evasive answers. Yet he seemed all that a mayor and father need be, for he was highly respected and ardently patriotic, and his two passions were fishing and jurisprudence. But finding that any mention of him roused Hildegarde's forest yearnings, I allowed Father to drop, and went on listening to the subjects which interest women, or answering questions about Oliver.

For Oliver was taking no more German lessons. However, he was in at the death, so to speak. It was, he explained to me afterwards, the interesting sight of Hildegarde registering emotion which had persuaded him to join us that day. She had arrived looking distraught. Her face was very pale, and blotched with weeping, and she had neglected to tong the five small curls on her forehead.

'Those Prewitts,' I said to myself, and asked what was the matter.

'My father—I had a letter this morning. He is in trouble.'

'I'm so sorry. What has happened? Is anyone ill?'

'He is in trouble. With the authorities. He is no longer Mayor.'

160

That comfortable, sensible man, who liked fishing and scratching his back—could he have poached? But it developed that it was not fishing but his other passion, jurisprudence, which had ruined him. He had, it appeared, fallen out with the authorities on some legal question, upholding against them some law which I could not disentangle from Hildegarde's explanation, except that it involved a right not to be searched without a warrant.

Oliver was quicker than I. More ruthless, too.

'Your father, then, is not a Nazi?'

Hildegarde turned about and looked at him like a shot rabbit. 'He is very patriotic. He . . . he . . .'

Like a shot, white rabbit. For her round face was bleached with fear, and her swollen eyelids and snub nose were a bright, ludicrous pink. It looked as though she would never be able to crawl back into the shelter of her forest.

Folk Cookery

WE had done our best with whist drives, socials, sixpenny hops, and a flower show to raise the money for a village nurse. Now the Ladies' Committee was planning how to make up our deficiencies.

'I feel strongly,' said Mrs. Beggerley Blatchford, 'that we should make a little book of Old English cookery—local lore, you know. And sell it at the post office and the railway station.'

We had rather expected her to feel like this. The B. B.s have a great deal of local and regional piety. Morris-dancers trample their lawn, their halls resound with sackbuts and fipple pipes, their cushions have hand-woven covers, rugged as granite.

'Elwin could print it for us,' she continued. 'And then we could charge much more for it. Hand-printed books always sell so nicely.' (Elwin is Mr. Beggerley Blatchford and owns a hand press.)

She was well away now. 'And the dear old people who contribute the recipes will feel they have done their share. That would be so nice, too. Suppose we each comb half a dozen?'

Most of our dear old people had been allotted to us when we remembered Mary Granby, absent from this meeting because her 'Eton Crop' haircut could be attended to only on Wednesdays, when that godlike Mr. Harry visited the county-town hairdresser.

'Well, now, who's left over to give Mrs. Granby?' said Mrs. Beggerley Blatchford. 'There's Mrs. Bugler, and Mrs. Trim, and Mrs. What's-Her-Name; you know, the good old thing with that dreadful husband. You know. He drinks, and was rather tiresome on election day.'

'Mrs. Sturmey?'

'Mrs. Sturmey. I think three would be quite enough for Mary Granby.'

On my way home I met the grocer's van, which nourishes us three times a week. The vanman likes conversation. He understood that it was with no bad intent that I asked him what staples he sold the most of.

'Bread and soap,' he replied unhesitatingly.

'And groceries?'

'Well, tinned salmon. We sell quite a lot of that. Then there's cereals. Here it's all Grape-Nuts, but over at Canon's Caudle it's Rolled Oats. Then there's cheese. And vinegar. And in summer it would surprise you how well these new lemonade crystals go.' He came running after me to say he had forgotten jam.

Different people demand different approaches. Jane Pitman, who was next on my list, is one of those who like a direct approach.

'Mrs. Beggerley Blatchford wants to know what your mother ate,' I said to her.

'Bread and scrape, Miss. Same as we.'

'Suppose your father happened to bring back a hare?'

'Sell it. Hare meat ain't wholesome for the likes of us, not while smells come out of chimney pots and tongues do wag in folkses' headses.'

I went next to Mrs. Goshawk, who, it developed, looked more sympathetically on the folklore of cookery. Old-fashioned ways had more to them, she said, and she had never had a tin-opener equal to the one she started married life with. Mrs. Rump, who happened to be borrowing a large-eyed needle from Mrs. Goshawk, agreed as to the virtues of times past. Look at the doctor's stuff we get now, she said. Old Dr. Faux had a pill that went through you like a ferret.

Miss Owles told me that if you rub a wart with a piece of raw beef, the beef will wither and so will the wart. But you couldn't do it with imported beef, she said. Mrs. Tizard, after long thinking, gave me a recipe for furniture polish, and a warning never to eat mushrooms after the first of October. Mrs. Cockaday gave me some medical advice of a kind which Elwin Beggerley Blatchford could never be asked to print; a recommendation to keep to dark teapots, for they made the tea stronger; and a large bunch of flowers.

When we came to pool our results with Mrs. Beggerley Blatchford, the total was disappointing: dark teapots make the strongest tea; chewing a clove will ease toothache; tough meat can be softened by burying it for a night and a day; sheep pastured in a churchyard don't make wholesome eating; a pint of warm beer stirred with a red-hot poker will cure the backache. And we had Miss Owles' cure for warts, and the recipes for Mrs. Tizard's furniture polish and Mrs. Tucker's grandmother's Kettle Broth, which was made by pouring boiling water on a sliced onion and some stale crusts. All the investigators had been told that mushrooms are poisonous after the first of October. 'There is the same belief in Yugoslavia. Isn't that fascinating?' said Mrs. Beggerley Blatchford. 'We must put in a little footnote about that. Folklore is so wonderfully universal.'

Mrs. Beggerley Blatchford's own discoveries were of a more Arcadian nature. They included bramble-tip cordial, cowslip pie, and candied hemlock. I, for one, did not believe in them. Mary Granby was the only one still to report.

'Now, Mrs. Granby,' said Mrs. Beggerley Blatchford, 'you are our last hope.'

'Well, I could do nothing with Mrs. Bugler, and Mrs. Trim was in bed with rheumatism, so I left her. But I've got these.' She opened a notebook. There was a great deal of pencil writing, in a singularly careful and childish hand. She read to us. '"Turnip Tantivy. Take three turnips, five pounds of raisins, a pound of the best butter, half a bottle of whisky, pepper and salt, mix and fry in a large iron frying pan that has a flavour of bloaters. When the turnips have taken up all the whisky, turn out into a pie dish."

'"Cottage Stew. Take some partridges, three or four; a pheasant, a fowl, a good hare, two pounds of the best beef-steak, green bacon in thick slices, vegetables, and herbs. Season richly and stew in a pot for three hours. Then pour in about a teapotful of port wine, and simmer for another hour."

'"Flummery. Cover the bottom of a deep basin with sliced quinces, strewed with nutmeg. Lay on them slices of Double Gloucester cheese. Then more quinces. Then more cheese. Go on doing this till the basin is two-thirds full. Pour in enough rich cream and old rum in equal quantities to cover them handsomely, and eat with cake."

'Mrs. Sturmey was out at work,' Mary Granby explained. 'But her husband was at home, and he dictated these recipes to me. He said this was how his old mother used to cook.'

'How very interesting,' answered Mrs. Beggerly Blatch-ford. 'Quite in the traditional spirit of English cook lore! But I wonder if we ought to include these recipes in our book. You see, Mrs. Granby, we hope our little book will be used by our dear villagers themselves. Perhaps these recipes would be a little ambitious—not quite in keeping with their simple tastes, dear souls!'

The meeting broke up soon after this, and Mrs. Beggerley Blatchford has not called the Ladies' Committee together since. Elwin is now hand-printing a booklet on Our Neolithic Remains.

Dieu et Mon Droit

W E had been perfectly satisfied with our Jubilee celebrations in the spring of '35. Every child under fourteen in our Dorset village had worn a golden paper crown. There had been a great deal to eat and drink, a bonfire, three accordion players and a cornet, and dancing till four in the morning.

However, some adverse comments broke out later on, especially among those whom most of us in the village call 'our betters.' Miss Woden, who plays the organ in church, regretted that Mr. Truebone, whose function it was to call for three cheers for King George after the largest rocket had gone up, should have seen fit to follow this by calling for three cheers 'for wold King Edward,' a sentiment greeted with equal enthusiasm. Rear Admiral Pinne (Retired) pointed out that the hired flags, believed by us to be flags of friendly foreign nations, were in reality quarantine flags, and must have indicated to any competent eye that our village, instead of rejoicing in a sovereign's Silver Jubilee, was announcing simultaneous outbreaks of cholera, plague, and yellow fever. And Miss Pinne, who is trying to make us Scout-conscious, discovered by inquiry that seventy per cent of the children were under the impression that the Jubilee was in honour of our postmistress, who is also our oldest inhabitant, and who was the person selected to hand out to the children the Jubilee souvenir mugs.

Our betters decided that any future celebrations must be of a more guided nature, and they undertook to do the guiding. There was scarcely time for them to do much about the Royal Funeral, but they got to work good and early on the Coronation. Everything was planned: the speakers, the decorations, every item of our behaviour, from the opening fanfare by Scouts and Brownies to the hour of 11:30 p.m., when we were to leave off dancing. The arrangements were sealed and concluded at a village meeting early in November.

Then came the news of the Abdication. It reached us by Mr. Pigeon, the mail-carrier. 'King has abdicated,' he said, 'and all the trains are late.'

We were standing in front of the post office. It was a foggy day, and we felt pretty melancholy. We felt for the Pinnes, too. 'The poor Pinnes won't be able to hold up their heads,' mused Mr. Pigeon, 'after all the trouble they've took over Coronation.'

I said there might still be a Coronation.

''Twon't be the same to them,' asserted Mr. Pigeon. 'Admiral loved that young man like a son.'

'Doesn't seem like Christmas now,' mourned Mrs. Pigeon.

While we were discussing whether the handsome young man on the grocer's presentation calendar was meant for King Edward or King George, a notice appeared in the post-office window:

VILLAGE MEETING

A meeting will be held to discuss the revision of the arrangements for the Coronation on Jan. 27th at 7:30. It is hoped all possible will attend. Brenda Pinne, Hon. Sec.

We hold our village meetings in the school. It is a melancholy building, with Gothic windows looking out on to the churchyard. Mr. Pretty, our esteemed blacksmith, was in the chair. He looked careworn. Miss Pinne, the Admiral's daughter, was beside him.

In the front row of chairs was Mrs. Pretty, looking steadfastly at Miss Pinne. They had fallen out pretty sharply over the question of whether Stanley Pretty should become a Scout or no. Mrs. Pretty had won, but she had not been as magnanimous as a victor should be.

It was a comment on the sad vicissitudes of life that the

minutes of the previous meeting should record the obsolete
arrangements for the Coronation. When Mr. Pretty came
to the words 'It was agreed that Admiral Pinne should undertake to order fifty-three souvenir mugs,' a sigh and a
shaking of heads went through the audience. After the
minutes, Mr. Pretty said a few words. A man of just mind
and a compassionate nature, he conveyed to us that in his
opinion both the abdicated and the succeeding monarch
had personal merits and much to bear. When he had
referred once or twice to 'the late King Edward,' Miss Pinne
leaned forward and whispered sharply, 'The Duke of
Windsor.' Mr. Pretty went on to give a few kind words to
Queen Elizabeth and then, his eye resting on Mrs. Pretty,
expressed a hope that the late Duke Edward might also in
time know the comfort of a domesticated fireside.

The Admiral, the Vicar, and Miss Woden drew down
their upper lips. Miss Pinne ejaculated, 'Heaven forbid!'

'I beg your pardon?' said Mrs. Pretty.

'And so, ladies and gentlemen,' concluded the chairman,
'we are met here tonight — and I think we may congratulate
ourselves on a very full attendance, though I do observe a
few absent faces — to thrash out, so to say, this little business
of revising the Coronation.'

The Admiral had now released his upper lip, and spoke.
'Some of our previous arrangements, of course, can stand.
Others will need certain modifications. We must not lose
sight of the fact that in this Coronation we shall be rejoicing
in the thought that beside our gracious King we shall have
our gracious Queen.'

We listened to the sad noise of the rain falling on the
tombstones.

'Such a welcome thought!' said Mrs. Pinne to Miss
Woden, in a stage undertone.

'I suppose,' said Mr. Truebone, 'that will mean
modifying the mugs.'

'The previous mugs,' said the Admiral, 'must, of course,
be jettisoned. But that need not trouble us. I have heard
from the makers, and I understand that they will be
168

prepared to take them back again, free of charge, provided we buy the new mugs from the same firm.'

A considerable whispering and shuffling now arose among the backward chairs. Ignoring it, Miss Pinne said, 'And here is a specimen of the *new* mug. I feel sure we shall all like to look at it.'

'Here!' exclaimed Mrs. Pretty. 'I want that Edward mug, if you please! I don't want to disappoint *my* child. He's a patriotic child, whatever some people may say.' And she glared at Miss Pinne.

Meanwhile the whispering had swelled to a tumult, and one could hear such phrases as 'Worth five times the money already,' 'Not for love or money,' 'Why, it will be historical by the time the child's grown up.'

Then, out of the tumult, voices aimed themselves at Miss Pinne.

'Please, Miss, will you put down my Eddie and my Doris and my Sheila and my Alice for Edward mugs? They've set their hearts on them.'

'And my Doris and my Jimmy too, Miss, if it's all the same to you.'

'My Billy and my Alice and my George, Miss Pinne.'

'Mrs. Lockett, two George mugs?' said Miss Pinne hopefully.

'No, Miss. Two Edwards, Please.'

'My Harry and my Hazel, Miss.'

'My Ruby.'

'My Ronald and my Bobby and my Alan and my Suzy.' Miss Pinne's pencil was twitching like summer lightning.

'I think we must have a show of hands,' said Mr. Pretty. 'Will those mothers who wish for Edward mugs for their children please put up their hands?'

Hands went up all over the room.

'Now those in favour of the George mugs.'

Three hands went up, two of them gloved.

Once again there was silence, and we listened to the noise of the rain falling on the tombstones. Mr. Truebone got up and slouched to the door.

'Perhaps,' said Mr. Pretty, 'the best expedient would be for the children to have both mugs.'

'My Cuthbert don't want no George mug,' said Mrs. Lockett.

'Come to that,' said Mr. Lockett, 'why should they have mugs at all? Can't a child drink out of a cup?'

Mrs. Pigeon recalled that at an earlier meeting some had been in favour of medals rather than mugs. Would it be a good plan to go back to medals? Mrs. Nokes said that you might as well give poison to a baby as a medal, for it would be sure to swallow it. Mrs. Lockett added that even if you put the medal away till the child was old enough to appreciate it, ten to one you'd mislay it.

Meanwhile a strategic notion was enlightening the Admiral. We saw him conferring with Mrs. Pinne and Miss Woden, with much nodding of heads. The notion was unfolded to the Vicar, who then nodded also.

'The thought has just struck me,' said the Admiral, 'that we might find the way out of our difficulties by quite a fresh alternative. How about a book?'

There was a dumbfounded silence among the Edward faction, but Miss Woden exclaimed, 'What a good idea! So much better than a mug. One never comes to the end of a book.'

'And the babies could not hurt themselves on it,' added Miss Pinne. 'The tots would enjoy the pictures.'

'Of our King and our Queen, and of the Empire. I often think we do not think enough about our Empire,' said Mrs. Pinne.

'Admiral,' said the Vicar, 'you have hit on the very thing! The Admiral proposes that since mugs are not universally acceptable, each child shall receive a book. I second that proposal.'

Mr. Pretty was just about to put it to a vote (and though no one wanted books, the unanimity of our betters was so compelling that probably books would have been carried) when Mr. Truebone slouched dreamily back again.

'About they mugs,' he began.

'We are now discussing books,' said the Vicar suavely.

'About paying for them, I mean,' continued Mr. Truebone. 'They Edwards, they won't be taken back unless we have they Georges. And 'tisn't all of us, seemingly, as wants a George.'

'Looks as though we should have paid for mugs and not have them,' mused Mr. Pigeon.

'It's an awkward consideration,' said the chairman.

While we considered, Mrs. Nokes was heard saying to Mrs. Wally that it was a pity the mugs had been bought so previous. Mrs. Wally replied that it was a pity, too, that they had changed the kings. It made such a lot of awkwardness.

Mr. Nokes asked how much the books would cost. The Admiral said, 'We need not trouble about that, my friends. Mrs. Pinne and I will be delighted to pay for the books.'

'And so,' said Miss Woden, 'thanks to Admiral Pinne, we are wafted out of the little difficulty.'

'No, us aren't!' shouted Mr. Nokes. 'For what about the money that's gone on the Edwards we're not to have?'

'Mugs is what we wanted, and mugs is what we should have,' said Mrs. Pretty, raising her voice.

'Mugs is what we'll be if we pay for them and don't get them,' added Mr. Lockett.

Everyone began to clamour for mugs.

'Them as wants mugs put up their hands!' cried Mrs. Pretty. A forest of hands appeared. 'There! That's carried. We want mugs.'

'Very well,' said the Admiral. 'But let me make one thing clear. We cannot celebrate the Coronation of King George with mugs bearing a portrait of the Duke of Windsor. If you want mugs, you must have the correct mugs.'

'It's Edward mugs we want!'

'Edward mugs, they Edward mugs!'

The unhappy Mr. Pretty, sweating heavily, was thumping for silence with an ink bottle.

'Ladies and gentlemen, ladies and gentlemen, *please!* May I suggest a kind of a compromise? Since this

171

Coronation is taking place under, so to speak, rather invidious circumstances, can't we give a certain measure of appreciation to both parties?'

'Hear, hear,' said Mr. Truebone.

'I propose that we give each child a George mug —'

'But my Eddie and my Doris and my Sheila —'

'And an Edward mug also.'

Mr. Truebone seconded. The proposal was carried. Mrs. Pinne rose to her feet. 'Oh, very well!' she said. 'But I tell you this. *You can pay for your Edwards yourselves.*'

Mr. Pretty asked if there was any other business. But our betters were already gathering themselves up to go. Mr. Pretty and Mr. Truebone and I stayed behind to put back the chairs and extinguish the oil lamps. Mr. Truebone had given Mr. Pretty a cigarette, and they were talking about seed potatoes. Outside was the rain, and the shuffle of feet, and the noise of the Admiral's car and the Vicar's car being started up. As I went by, I heard Mrs. Pinne's voice, louder than the growls of a reluctant self-starter, saying the word 'Bolsheviks'.

A Queen Remembered

I T was New Year's Eve — and so long ago that I cannot remember the date of the year. We had finished our dinner and were drinking coffee in the upper room when we fell to making New Year's resolutions — a calm process, since we had often made them before. We must keep a register of books we'd lent, and consult it in order to reclaim them; we must tidy the garage, throw away all the old paintpots, buy some new wastepaper baskets, invite the Harrisons to a meal.

'One thing we must do,' said Valentine with decision. 'We must buy some peat blocks. We always talk about peat fires. We never have them. This year we will.'

'But where from? Coal merchants don't sell peat blocks. Peat just means azaleas in Dorset.'

'Yes, there's another thing we must have. When does one plant azaleas?'

'Not till the frost is out of the ground.'

'Good. That leaves tomorrow. Tomorrow we will drive into Somerset and buy a load of peat.'

It was stimulating to have a New Year's resolution which could be put into effect at once. On New Year's Day we emptied the hold of the car, studied the road map, and drove towards Sedgemoor.

We had learned from other pursuits of the attainable that in the West of England it does not do to ask point-blank for information. It is proverbial that if a stranger in a car halts to ask a pedestrian the way to such-and-such, the pedestrian cups a deaf ear, puts on a grieved, thwarted expression, and walks away; or replies, after the question

173

has been repeated several times, that he really can't say, he is a stranger himself. In neither case is this true. The cupped ear catches every word you say, the stranger is a hardened inhabitant. It is you, not your inquiry, which is of interest. As they don't like to appear inquisitive they learn what they can about you by observation. Only when you have acquired a certain mossiness as a familiar object can you expect to be answered. Knowing this, we entered a roadside inn called the Volunteer and asked for bread and cheese and two half pints of draught beer. There we sat, waiting for the moss to grow and seeing from the window how incoming customers stopped for a good look at our car.

A bold spirit addressed us. 'Come from far?'

'From near Dorchester.'

'Ah.'

'We are looking for somewhere where we can buy peat. Do you happen to know—' There was a disclaiming silence. I went no further.

A voice at the back of the room said, 'What about Bert Cary?'

We said nothing. We had not been addressed.

'Or young Damon?'

'Maybe he might. But he's in Bridgwater on Fridays.'

'Always is. With his lorry.'

'What about his mother, though?'

Opinion seemed pretty evenly divided as to whether Mrs. Damon might or mightn't.

All this time a peat fire was noiselessly burning on the hearth, filling the room with its smell of mouldered summers.

Valentine now struck like a falcon. 'Where does Mrs. Damon live?'

Startled into compliance, the customers of the Volunteer directed us to Mrs. Damon's house, which we couldn't miss if we turned to the left a couple of miles or so short of the old pumping station.

'Your hair smells of peat already,' said Valentine as I got

into the car. 'Peat and beer.'

It has always seemed to me that skies are coloured by the soil beneath. We had begun our journey under the sharp forget-me-not blue of chalk. Now we travelled under a web of smokey bronze and cobalt. The road was ditched on either side and pollard willows grew along the banks. It was a landscape in which it was impossible to judge distance. Its measure was duration, not miles. We had driven for a long way before a huddle of bricks and timbers told us that we should have turned off to the left a couple of miles before. We drove back and took the turning into a narrow track. Like the road we had left, it was straight, ditched, willowed, and featureless, except for being deeply rutted. Encouraged by this assurance of young Damon's lorry, we drove on and on. A hen crossed the track.

'Where there is a hen there is a woman,' I said. 'It can't be far off now.'

'It looked to me like a lost hen,' said Valentine. I replied that it couldn't be lost unless it had a home to stray from.

We had branched from hens to the dubious efficacy of scholastic logic when Mrs. Damon's house started up behind the willows. The ruts led us over a plank bridge into a yard with some sheds standing about in it. They looked casual and dilapidated. Not so the woman who came out of the house. She was tall and thin. She held herself erect and wore a long white apron. Her grey hair was fastened in a neat knob.

She was Mrs. Damon.

I explained. She listened to me and looked at Valentine. This was nothing out of the common. I continued to explain and Mrs. Damon continued to look. Seeing that I was getting nowhere, Valentine also began to explain. Mrs. Damon came back to real life, smoothed her apron, and asked how much peat we wanted. As much as we could get into the car, Valentine said. Mrs. Damon glanced at the two-seater. With an air of indulgent gravity, she opened the peat shed and hauled out a sack,

175

remarking that we would get more in if we packed them by hand. Together we packed the peats into the hold and behind the seats, and Mrs. Damon's apron remained as white as ever, and her lips fluttered as she kept her count. All this took some time, as she and Valentine were both determined to get in as many peats as possible. When the last blocks had been fitted in, we stood back and surveyed each other, as fellow-workers do. Suddenly Mrs. Damon said to Valentine, 'You don't come from hereabout, do you?'

'From Dorset.'

In that sombre, brooding landscape, Dorset seemed far distant; but not distant enough to satisfy Mrs. Damon's conjecture. 'Not born there, though?'

'No, I was born in London.'

'That's what I thought. Whereabouts in London?'

'In Brook Street.'

'Just so. Runs into Park Lane, doesn't it? The moment you got out of the car, I said to myself, "That's the West End." It was something I never thought to see again.'

'So you're a Londoner, too?'

'Not born. But I was in service there for twelve years. The best years of my life. It was a wonderful place—two in family and seven servants kept. Porchester Terrace. Then I went too far on Armistice Night, and had to marry him, and came down here. And here I've been ever since. I suppose I wouldn't know London again if I saw it now.'

'The Park's much the same—though if you saw some of the riders in Rotten Row they'd be a surprise to you.'

'Never is what it used to be—that's what they say about London, you know. Mrs. Jobling, she was the housekeeper, used to talk about her first place. There was a golden fountain in the hall, and when the family had their dinner parties and receptions it was turned on and sprayed out eau de cologne. But that was in the old Queen's days.'

'Did you ever see her?'

'No. But I've still got my Diamond Jubilee mug they gave at the school treat. All these years I've treasured it.

And I've left it in my will that it's to be buried with me.'

A moist wind had risen and swayed the willow boughs. Mrs. Damon's hens were gathering round her. It was a strange place in which to be hearing about golden fountains, I thought. Mrs. Damon was talking on.

'A good Queen, if ever there was one. And over and above, she was a good woman. And the faithfulest of widows. I never look at my mug but I think of her driving to the Albert Memorial. Every afternoon she drove out in her closed carriage, with a lady-in-waiting or a princess beside her, drove from Buckingham Palace along Knightsbridge as far as the Albert Memorial. And there the carriage would stop, and she'd look at it—look at it with all her heart and soul. And then she'd signal and be driven back, hiding her face behind a white handkerchief with a black border. There's love for you. There's faithfulness.'

'Yes, indeed.'

We paid, and drove away. After a pause, I began:

> And out of his grave there grew a rose,
> And out of her grave a briar . . .

Valentine took it up:

> And ever they grew and ever they grew
> Till they could grow no higher,
> And twined themselves in a true lovers' knot
> For all folk to admire.

Forgetting our errand, forgetting our route, we marvelled at this encounter with the authentic voice of balladry which had installed Lytton Strachey's Victoria, Victoria of the sneers, among the Good Queens of legend: Eleanor of the Crosses, Queen Anne of the lace, Berengaria who sucked the poisoned wound, Philippa whose great belly shielded the burghers of Calais. Talking of these, speculating about Mrs. Damon, we lost our way twice over in the gathering dusk before we reached home.